Play Jimmy Roselli

A Novel

By Kenneth J. Uva

On a sunny fall Sunday, the kind of crisp clear day when my city was filled with activity, the kind of day my late wife loved so much, I found myself alone. The woman I had been seeing was out of town for a few days so my usual companion on this perfect day was not around. Not wanting to waste such a day, I decided to venture downtown to Ground Zero. The area was now a tourist attraction filled with singles, couples, and groups of all colors and languages. I walked through the new transportation hub that looked like it belonged in a futuristic movie, and took the voyage to the top of the new 1 World Trade Center. From that height and on that clear day, I viewed my city laid out below. This is the city where I was born, worked, and lived most of my life. My thoughts drifted back to September 11, 2001, the day my subway stopped due to an announced "police activity" at the World Trade Center. At 42nd Street, a man got on and said to anyone in the vicinity that two hijacked planes crashed into the World Trade Center. The E train terminated there so, of course, it did not go to its terminus but, instead, let us off at 34th Street. When I hit the street, I could see smoke billowing from both towers. I called my office that was less than a mile downtown to tell them I was on the way. Then, I heard shrieks in the background and was told that one of the towers had just collapsed. I knew my city and my country would never be the same.

Across the street from the World Trade Center, at 90 Church Street, is a federal office building. My mother worked there in the Navy Department during World War II. Memories began to flood through my head as I thought of the long journey of my life, the thought of my mother as a young woman, my father as a young sailor in the South Pacific, and of their parents, brothers and sisters and of their generation and of my generation and of all of the journeys from various places both geographical and in the heart and mind that make us who we are.

Chapter 1. Heaven. And Brooklyn

"Is Grandpa behind there," I asked, pointing to the curtains behind the altar of St. Anthony's Church. The church was typical of Catholic churches built in Italian neighborhoods in the early 20th Century. The interior was painted light blue, with white trim, with paintings and wall hangings that imitated Renaissance art, or perhaps were copies, with painted statues of saints, a crucifix with red wounds, rows of candles, and the Stations of the Cross, all reminders of the suffering and death of Jesus and other martyrs.

Sitting between my mother, Carmella, and her eldest sibling, Aunt Rose, I was told that we were at church for Grandpa. I was not quite four years old, but had been witnessing a great deal of activity around me lately. I didn't understand what was going on but knew something important and something very sad, was happening.

A few days before, my mother, father, aunts, and uncles entered our apartment in a frightening array of sobbing, loud crying, and hysterics. When I asked why everyone was crying, my mother told me that Grandpa went to heaven. I didn't exactly know where heaven was but knew that Grandpa was gone. The man who I woke up every morning would no longer be in his bed when I arose every morning.

I lived with my mother, and my father Peter, with Grandpa Vito on the second floor of the house in Brooklyn that Vito owned. There was a ritual every morning as I greeted him to meet the day and had long conversations with the old gentleman about farms, and cows, and boats, and about what a good boy I was. "Brian, he talks so good, he's gonna be a lawyer when he grows up," he would tell Carmella, who everyone called Millie. In the days before daycare and preschool and Gymboree, children stayed home with their mothers. For me, that meant being home with Vito also. I was told later that Vito was very proud of me. I remember that he would take me for walks to the corner near the candy store where he would buy the Italian newspaper and chat with other older Italian men, mostly from Naples, Sicily and other parts of Italy south of Rome. Of course, at the time, I didn't know where these men were from but even then I knew there were people around who spoke a different language or spoke English but sounded different from my parents, aunts, uncles and cousins. Vito was indulgent in the small ways that was a treat for me, by buying ice cream or lollipops, in the age before people knew that sugar was a bad thing. Favorite purchases include a bunch of lollipops tied together with a rubber band and ice cream in Dixie Cups, to be eaten with a flat wooden spoon and contained in a cup, making it easy for a small boy to eat without making a mess.

It really hit me in the gut that Grandpa was not coming back when men came to take away his bedroom furniture. I remember that the knobs on the drawers were like marbles as the furniture was headed out the door for Uncle Louie's apartment across the street. It mattered little that the furniture stayed in the family. I only knew that Grandpa was gone forever. For the first time in my life, at not quite four years old, I was sad.

In Brooklyn, in the mid-1950s, among Italian-Americans, mourning was a very ritualized process. And God forbid you broke a rule. Efforts to comfort those who suffered the loss were rote and perfunctory. Sure, everyone said how sorry they were. "He's in heaven now." "He is with your mother," were what I heard not understanding what these words really meant or that they could have been written on cue cards when visiting the grieving family. A few people came from out of town but did not stay in hotels. They were expected to be put up in the houses of the grieving family. Not only did mother have to deal with the loss of her father, she also had to accommodate and wait on, and cook for, a bunch of people I didn't know from some branch of the family from Boston. She was twenty-nine years old, eight months pregnant, had lost her mother only two years before, had a young child, and now had to serve demanding houseguests in a small apartment. As I learned as I grew up, there were codes of conduct associated with rites of passage, many of which added to the burdens of those who were supposed to be comforted. God forbid anyone violated these strictures. People will talk about you, which they did anyway.

"Mommy, a man took my pillow last night." She said nothing even though her child's personal space was intruded upon by a person he didn't know. Even at that young age, I felt violated. No one took my bed, but a stranger taking my pillow felt wrong. Of course, I could not articulate that my personal space was compromised but I was really bothered by this. Years later, when she was far enough away from these duties to express her feelings, Mother complained that in such a sad time for her, no one was there to make anything easier. When her mother was home dying of cancer a few years before, she did it all, even though other siblings and their wives were within walking distance. "Rhoda would come to wash the breakfast dishes," she said, "but that was it." I could feel the bitterness, but understood that in that time and in that place, a daughter did was she was supposed to do, one of which was to keep up appearances at all times, so no one would talk about you. One afternoon, a few years after Grandpa died, people from an out-of-town branch of the family showed up unannounced. The protocol was to pretend that she was happy to see them and, of course, serve coffee and cake. I was about seven at the time and she sent me to the store around the corner to buy a cake. Apparently, I didn't know a prepackaged chocolate cake with white frosting was not appropriate for the occasion. Mother had a look of disgust and said "Ewww...Is this what you bought?" and made a sound that is difficult to reproduce in writing. Appearances were everything so sending a seven-year old on an emergency mission focused on the seven-year-old's failure rather than on four people who dropped in unexpectedly. It was so important what other people thought, that she did not think about hurting my feelings with regard to something I thought was the right thing. How did I know what kind of cake was appropriate for a random afternoon drop in?

"There were always people over the house in those days," according to Mother. My mother would cook spaghetti, my father served the home made wine, there was bread and that was enough to keep everybody happy. In those days a bowl of macaroni was a big deal. My uncle Ralph wanted some meat so he trapped a little sparrow on the garage roof and broke its neck and cooked it. How much meat could he get off that tiny bird? I hated him for that."

"Nobody had much so my uncle and a few others would drop in at dinner time. If someone was there, you had to feed them. They would fuss over what a great meal the spaghetti was, drink coupla glasses of wine, and compliment my mother by calling her Saint Veronica. It was the depression and people didn't have much to eat," Mother recounted. "None of them worked," my father said, "They spent their lives hustling for a meal." As a child, it was hard to understand not having a good, full meal at dinner time, a sandwich for lunch, and whatever cookies I wanted, and a glass of milk to wash them down.

According to family consensus, Grandpa Vito was a good man. Mother told me that he considered himself an American once he got to these shores. That wasn't the case for everyone who came from Italy. One neighbor from around the corner lost her husband in WWI when he went back to fight for Italy. "It is my duty, he told his wife," Mother said. "Yeah, and Pascalina had to raise two kids without a husband."

Peter's father, Giorgio, was a big fan of Mussolini until WWII broke out and three of his sons served. One of the family on my grandmother's side, the rich relatives, owned a funeral home in the neighborhood. When the Italians conquered Ethiopia in the 1930s, there was a local parade in celebration. An African-American man who worked in the funeral home was seated in a casket, with a sign that said

"Qui giance Abyssinia." (Here lies Abyssinia.) The ties to the old country were not yet cut.

Vito would argue with the men who claimed that Benito was good for Italy because he gave Italians pride and brought back the glory of the Roman Empire. "Italians, they crazy to be with Germany. Italians are no fighters. They all gonna get killed and Italy gonna burn down. America is my country." When the Italian Air Armada of seaplanes few to the United States in the 1930s, Air Marshall Balbo was treated like a hero. Giorgio, a former soldier in the Italian army, was proud of this show of military prowess. Vito, however, said, "Next time, those airplanes gonna have bombs."

"The Italian men would come to the house and argue about Italy," Mother said. "My uncle said how Mussolini was good for Italy. Grandpa said that he was going to start a war and thousands of Italians would get killed. My uncle said that Italy has a big navy and many airplanes and would win a war." "Who is Italy gonna fight, America?," he said. He said that Italy is getting ready for war. He knew that because the family upstairs came from Italy but their teenage son could not come because men of military age were not allowed to leave Italy. "They not letting young men leave Italy 'cause they need them for the army," Grandpa reportedly said. "So many of them gonna get killed. I feel sorry for Pepine and Nino."

Still, they all kept their connections with whoever was left in Italy. Mother's family came from the region inland from Naples. When Vesuvius erupted in 1944, panic spread in the neighborhood over the safety of their families. Since the war was on, communication with Italy was very spotty. "My mother was so worried about her aunt and cousins that she cried for weeks until we found out they were OK," Mother told me. "Everybody in the neighborhood had some family there. A lotta candles were lit in the church."

There was great concern in the neighborhood throughout World War II, especially when the allies invaded Sicily and fought their way north up the boot. "My mother cried thinking about the war and what could be happening in Italy," according to my mother. "In those days," my father added, "people here didn't know how bad the fighting was over there. Naples was bombed, people were starving. After Italy left the war, the Germans dug in and fought for every mile. My friend Ralph was in Italy. He said it was hell, between the Germans and the mud. He was in the battle of Cassino. The Germans were on the mountain and thousands of guys were killed trying to get them off. We even had to bomb an old monastery on the top of the mountain because the Germans were using it to shoot artillery into the valley. Ralph came home OK but lost a lot of friends."

Mother would tell very positive stories about her father. " When he was in school Grandpa's teacher told him that there was nothing more he could teach him, so he would have to go to the next level of school. His father deserted the family to go to America. The teacher wrote to him for money for Grandpa to go to school. He never got an answer so that was the end of his education," Mother said one day to me. "You complain about school but Grandpa woulda done anything to go to school. How come you don't like school, anyway? You're the smartest boy in the class."

As a child, I had no way of knowing anything about my grandparents other than what my parents told me. Since reputation was of utmost importance in the family and in the neighborhood, every story had a spin so that each family member was presented in the best light. "After Grandpa stopped going to school," Mother said, "he was an apprentice to a shoemaker." "What's an apprentice?" I asked. She continued, "An apprentice is a young man who works for an older man who teaches him his trade. In Italy, a shoemaker made shoes, not like in America. Here we call them shoemakers but they only fix shoes."

"He made a beautiful pair of shoes for my mother. Everybody in the town admired them so people wanted him to make shoes for them.

The man he worked for said, 'You are as good as me now. You can't be my apprentice anymore.' " "Did he open his own store?" I asked. "No," replied Mother, "he went to America to find his father."

"He came to this country," she continued, "but never found his father. He decided to stay in this country and had to work to save enough money to bring my mother here. He went to Pennsylvania and opened a small business making shoes. Finally he sent for my mother. By that time, Aunt Rose was born. So, Momma came on the boat with an infant, and with her mother in law." Even as a child, I realized that my mother's stories were usually sad, about separation, loss, and deprivation. That is probably why my DNA usually told me that the glass is half empty, and that there is always a cloud to obscure the silver lining.

The coming to America story had a sad beginning. "Momma came to Ellis Island, where the boat left the people who came from Europe." "Where is Ellis Island?," I asked. "In New York, right near the Statue of Liberty. Momma was with a baby and Grandpa's mother. She didn't know where she was or where she was going. Then, Grandpa's mother had something wrong with her eyes so they kept her in Ellis Island. They put Grandma and Aunt Rose on a train to where, she didn't know. She cried the whole way. She thought she would never see Grandpa again. After a long ride, the train stopped in Pennsylvania, and she saw Grandpa waiting for her at the station. She said 'It was like I saw God.' "

I learned later that it was common to keep people in quarantine in Ellis Island for minor health problems. Vito went there and sprung his mother.

As a child, I listened to all these stories. As a child, however, I couldn't really relate to what it meant to be so scared that you might never see your loved ones again, having no resources, knowledge of your surroundings or language, or reason for hope. Many years later, visiting the museum that Ellis Island had become, armed with a lifetime of experience, I teared up frequently at the displays and the film. "Daddy, are your crying?" asked my daughter Zoe. This was the history of my family, and the families of people I knew. Necessity forced them to come to a strange new world, hoping for a better life. For many, they never again saw those they left behind. I thought of the grandmother who died before I was a year old, as a frightened young woman with an infant and an old woman, thrust into a strange place, along with thousands of others, not knowing what was going to happen next. It was a long journey from our roots in Italy to becoming a real American.

"If they were in Pennsylvania, how come they came to Brooklyn," I asked Mother. "In those days there was the Black Hand, Italian gangsters that made people pay them or they would beat them up or burn their businesses. Grandpa didn't want to keep paying them so he left to come here."

Grandma did not adapt well to her new land. Vito had a measure of success in the 1920s with a wicker furniture business. "He would soak the wicker and when it was soft, he made it into furniture. Rich people bought it for their porches and sun rooms on Bushwick Avenue, around Highland Park, and in Brooklyn Heights," Mother told me. "He made good money. He bought this house and we even had a car." Curious at the thought of Grandma and Grandpa, or anyone of their generation actually driving around, I asked if the family went on trips with the car. "Once, we drove to Atlantic City. Grandpa wanted to stay over in a hotel. Grandma said 'I gotta sleep in somebody else's bed?' so we drove back home. Anyway, in the Depression, nobody bought that kind of furniture any more and he had to close the business in the store downstairs. The government used the store to hand out relief food and shovels and stuff for work projects. They used to send hams upstairs but Momma didn't know what to do with them."

My paternal grandfather, Giorgio, had a different motivation for coming to America. As did many young men in Italy of modest means and prospects, he joined the army, then the *carabinieri,* the national police force. "My father was a very proud man," Peter told me. "He was stationed in St. Peter's Square, and he told me about the enormous church, and the Pope and all the cardinals, priests and nuns he saw every day. That's how I got my name."

When I was an adult, and, arguably, able to bear such a story, Peter told me of how his father once caught a priest "giving it to a woman" behind some columns near the Vatican. Later, when I visited Vatican City, I wondered where the Bernini columns offered enough privacy for someone to risk a sexual encounter. "He turned him in. After that he had no respect for the Church. A priest is just a man, my father would say." I thought that considering the stories about priests that came to light much later, at least this priest was giving it to an adult woman. I also wondered, with his attitude toward the Church, why he named his son after the center of Roman Catholicism. Peter explained that Giorgio admired Saint Peter, the person, not the institution that used his name. At that point, I became very sorry that he never met the old man.

"My mother's family was well off," Peter told me. "They owned a butcher shop and had servants. She came to this country because, one day, my father said to pack up, we're going to America. My father's sister was coming here, so my father wanted to come too. My mother had a good life in Italy, but thanks to my father, she came here and hardly ever left the house. She would get lost if she walked a few blocks from home. After she came here, she never saw her family again."

When I was old enough to hear more details, I learned that my grandfather's sister had to leave Italy in a hurry. ""Her landlord wanted to have sex with her," Peter told me. "She refused. They told her that she could not refuse a rich man and that the local gangsters would rape her for breaking the rules. So, she packed right away and left the town, and booked passage to New York. My mother had to go, of course, even though she was happy where she was."

Peter and his brothers would get teary eyed when they talked about Momma. Giovanna, like most women who came from Italy to East New York in the early 1900s, spent a life in the kitchen, cooking modest meals, washing clothes, and attending to her family, but to her husband first. Peter told me that their meals consisted of one dish. "We had pasta fazool or spaghetti. Maybe some chicken or meatballs on special occasions. She had to feed nine people. And Papa always got the first pick. He was the man of the house so he ate before anyone else."

"He was a barber," Peter continued. "He cut our hair, of course. One time, my brother Paul was fidgeting too much so he took his clippers and made the sign of the cross on his head. My mother yelled at him, which she never did. He realized what he did and tried to even the hair the best he could."

"I was always frustrated as a kid," Peter continued. "There were so many people in the house. Nobody noticed me. I had 4 older brothers, and two sisters. My father never played ball with me or took me to the park. I was on my own. One day, I was about 7. I took a tumblesauce off the stoop and hurt my head and nobody cared. I was so mad at everybody, I ran away from home, to Highland Park. I was gone all day. When I got hungry and came home, nobody knew I was gone. Another time, there was the feast in front of my house. My mother took me down to walk around. A guy said to me *'Piango mio caro cosi la mamma ti comprera un pallioncino.'* That meant cry, little boy so you mother will buy you a balloon. I cried and my mother took me upstairs."

"You think that I got toys at Christmas like you do? One year I wanted a toy car. I dreamed about it. I dreamed that on Christmas morning, it was right next to my bed. On Christmas morning they gave me a toy clock that I was playing with for a coupla weeks." "Didn't your older brothers think about getting you a present for Christmas,"

Mother asked? "Nah, they had their own lives. Christmas then wasn't like now. I hope you kids appreciate it."

My father's Christmas experiences motivated him to make my Christmas special. Even though his salary was modest at the time, I always remember those wonderful mornings with toys spread out under the tree. It helped that my mother saved one dollar a week at her bank's Christmas Club, a special account that paid no interest but provided the discipline for people of modest means to have money for the holidays.

To this day, the smell of pine trees brings me back to one particular Christmas. One of my many presents was a cavalry fort with interlocking metal pieces with painted logs, as those forts were pictured in movies. The set came with a headquarters building and numerous toy soldiers and Indians. One whiff of pine pointed to one special present even though there were many presents over many years.

It wasn't just the smell of pine that evoked the past. Christmas also meant special foods. Meat was not allowed in Christmas Eve so the air was filled with the aroma of frying fish. There was also a traditional family recipe of angel hair pasta in a garlic anchovy sauce. To add sweetness to the dish, prunes were put into the preparation. For the decades to come, members of the extended family would ask, "Did you have the prunes?"

The cooking, including such labor intensive foods like zeppoli, was Mother's effort, but the toys were the responsibility of my father, whose labor of love was to assemble the things he never had so that I did. Probably my favorite toy of all time was a red fire engine that I could sit in and peddle all over the block. It had two removable ladders and a bell with a string to allow me to ring it as I made my travels. Several decades later, I saw a tree ornament of that very fire engine. Of course, I bought it and have hung it on my tree ever since.

Mother took a different tone when talking about her childhood. She talked about the parties with her family, and the singing and dancing and how happy her house was. "Grandpa played the mandolin and everyone used to sing. We had so much fun."

She grew up in the house where she stayed after she was married and where I lived for several years. The special feature was a two-car garage that faced a broad thoroughfare, Atlantic Avenue. The garage roof one story above street level was made into what would pass for a penthouse in that neighborhood. Grandpa Vito built a covered picnic table that could seat maybe 20, especially with kids squeezed in Italian family style. At the far end, there was a concrete flower bed that extended from front to back, filled with red petunias and orange marigolds. At the wall facing the street were three huge concrete flower pots with evergreen plants. The total effect was an oasis in a shabby neighborhood and a mecca for us and any family members who stopped by, usually unannounced.

"We always had people over on the garage," Mother said. "Aunt Rose and her family came over all the time. We always had so much fun." "Your sister liked to come to get a free meal that she didn't have to cook, "Peter would respond. "Momma loved to cook for everybody. That's how I learned to make the gravy," Mother responded. As a young boy, I preferred my mother's version of the past. I liked the idea that my older cousins, all girls, and my uncles, aunts, and grandparents, were all partying in the years when they were waiting for me to be born.

I especially loved the stories about what a beautiful baby I was, according to Mother, and how people would stop her on the street to admire me. Of course, after I became a parent, I saw how people always stopped to admire infants in baby carriages. There were no mediocre infants, after all.

Yet, as I got older and could read between the lines, maybe everything wasn't as great as Mother made it out to be.

"You always have to talk nice. Say please and thank you," Mother said. "You want people to think you're a good boy." I learned that it was very important to care what people thought. After all, we lived in the same house where she grew up. One brother lived across the street and had a store on the ground floor of our house. Another brother lived two blocks away. Another lived five blocks away and visited every day after he finished his postal route. And his wife's aunt lived three doors away. There were many others who were related to our relatives on the spouses' side of the family so, in short, our little piece of Brooklyn had some of the qualities of a village in Italy. Everyone knew everyone else's business and everyone talked. You must never give anyone a reason to think you were less than perfect.

At that time, accepting of Mother's version of history and her spin to present to the world, I had no idea of the bad stuff that the family did not talk about, or even admit.

"Papa. Momma, is crying," twelve-year-old Millie said to her father. Momma had been acting strangely of late. Her temper was out of control. She threw the dog off the garage roof, injuring the poor pooch that never came near her again. She refused to cook causing Millie to pick up the slack for her father and brothers. She became prone to strange Italian curses and hardly got out of bed. As a good Catholic family, a decision was made to have her talk to a priest, the font of wisdom in an era and place that did not have therapists of any kind.

They met with the priest and Vito explained that Momma was acting strange, like she was possessed by the devil. The priest didn't take issue with the concept of possession but concluded, from the evidence that her behavior did not rise to that level. "Somebody has put a curse on her," the priest reasoned. His remedy was to make a novena, a nine-day ritual of prayers and devotion. So, for nine days, the family gathered at home, said prayers, lit candles, and dedicated the whole thing to the Blessed Mother. Despite carefully following the prescribed rituals, Momma's behavior remained the same.

The family had relatives in the steel mill region of Pennsylvania so they decided to send Momma there for a change of scenery. At home, the cooking and cleaning chores fell to Millie since boys didn't do such things. "I used to love to be sick," Mother said years later, "so my father would stay home and make me chicken soup."

After a month or so, it appeared that Momma regained her faculties enough to come home.

Young Millie had high standards and an agenda. She didn't use the coarse language like so many of the neighborhood girls. In fact, it was often said "She thinks who she is." She was a high school graduate in a time and place where that was not commonplace. She was a fine-looking, well-groomed young woman with good typing skills. During World War II she landed a job with the Navy Department. She worked in the Officers' Personnel Division. Due to the Navy traditions and hierarchy, this was no ordinary job. Naval officers were gentlemen too and the Navy treated them as such. So the Officers' Personnel Division was staffed by elite secretaries. I had seen pictures of the "girls" in that office. Every one of them was attractive and well dressed in the Betty Grable, Andrews Sisters style of the time. Miss Carter, the supervisor, required hats and gloves, no gum chewing, and the most refined deportment at all times.

The Navy Department was an eye opener for Millie. She worked in the Federal Building in lower Manhattan. So, every day, she rode the subway out of Brooklyn to "New York." She ate lunch with the other young working women at Schrafts on special occasions and the Horn and Hardart Automat on regular days. Sure, it wasn't Park Avenue. But it wasn't Brooklyn either. It was, for her, a world of what might be. A world where people dressed nicely, and spoke and acted with some "class."

"Grandma was so proud that Mommy didn't work in a factory. She would say *'Mia figlia lavora in un officio.'* That meant my daughter works in an office," according to my father..

"Miss Carter invited us to her house on Long Island in the summer. She lived in Roslyn. It was such pretty little house," according to Mother. "She had a small backyard with grass and beautiful flowers. I thought it was so nice to have a house in the country with nobody upstairs or downstairs who knew your business. There were no houses like that in Brooklyn. There were some private houses around here but they didn't have grass and they were close together. Germans lived in them."

"The people there were very refined," Mother went on. "Some of the girls even went to college. Nobody said 'ain't' or 'yeah.' The officers came in for their orders. They were all so handsome. You had to go to college to be an officer and they were real gentlemen. They usually had some time before had to go to their assignment so sometimes they hung around and talked to us. After work, I had coffee with a lieutenant. He was American, from Illinois. I never met anybody from that part of the country. I don't remember what town but it was a small town, not Chicago. I pictured it to look like a town in a movie, like where Andy Hardy lived. He wanted to see New York. He never was here before. The next night I took him to Times Square. The lights were dimmed during the war so German planes couldn't find the city but still I think all the lights and all the people made him dizzy. We saw a movie, and then went dancing at Roseland. He was very nice but that was it. He knew I had a boyfriend and that Daddy was in the Pacific. It wasn't romantic or anything but I knew he was homesick and I wanted to be nice to him because he was in the service. In those days, a lot of girls went out with servicemen coming through New York. Thousands of men shipped out from here and I guess we thought it was part of the war effort. My best friend, you know Chris, met Al when he was stationed here with the Coast Guard. He was from Mobile,

Alabama. I know that for some of the girls, when they went out with servicemen, it wasn't so innocent."

Mother didn't tell me the last part when I was a kid but I sure heard much about the good looks, fine speech, and good behavior of the men who came to her office. The thread of all of that to me was that all the good stuff came from going to college. "If you go to college, you can be an officer in the navy," Mother said. "After the navy, you could work in an office with a shirt and tie instead of a factory or driving a truck." One time, in the latter part of the 1950s we were driving on an overpass with commercial buildings along the street. From that height, we could see into second floor windows. In one of them, we saw a number of men gathered around a table of some sort. They all wore white shirts and ties. "I bet they make a hundred dollars a week, Mother observed.

One day, Mother took some suitcases out of a closet. These were of a typical style of the 40s, covered with smooth blue leather with a heavy brown leather trim. The initials read "CM." I asked why those letters were on her luggage. She said that before she was married, her name was Carmela Mazzola. That was the first time I knew her real name. "Millie is short for Carmela but I hate the name Carmela. It's so old fashioned, like I just came over on the boat."

"My birthday is on the Feast of Our Lady of Mount Carmel so that is how I got my name. Momma made me promise before she passed away that I would go to the feast in Brooklyn, so we are going on my birthday in a few weeks." And so we did. She and I took the subway to a neighborhood in Brooklyn that was more Italian than ours. There were all the trappings of an Italian church feast, vendors selling balloons and other small toys, booths with Italian food. We didn't buy any of the street food since she said she could make any of that and the food on the street was not as good as hers anyway. The main focus of the feast, however, was the *Giglio,* a large tower lifted by what seemed to be a hundred strong men and carried through the streets. Later I learned that the tower commemorated another event in Italian history but by the time Mother took me to the feast, it was combined with the Feast of Our Lady of Mount Carmel.

I did not enjoy the journey. It was just too Italian for this American boy. There were too many old ladies in black dresses and people crossing themselves or pounding their breasts. Exactly the surroundings that made me more convinced than ever that I was an American, not Italian.

In a world where boys were named Anthony, Vincent, Frank, Joseph, and Robert, after ancestors named Antonio, Vincente, Francesco, Giuseppe, and Roberto, I was named Brian. No one in the entire neighborhood was named Brian. From what she told me about her own name, I figured she wanted me to have a name that didn't sound Italian, probably so my passport out of the Brooklyn would be stamped upon exit. Of course, at that age, I didn't think about any of this.

My world at three and four was one of being the special boy. Of seeing aunts, uncles and cousins every day. Of watching black and white TV on a small screen. My first crush was on Princess SummerFallWinterSpring on *The Howdy Doody Show.* My first fear was of the puppet Poison Zoomack on *The Rootie Kazootie Club.*

It was through TV that I learned that real Americans did not live in railroad apartments above a store in Brooklyn, in a neighborhood of attached wood frame and shingle houses with front stoops. In the context of our neighborhood, our apartment was quite nice. We were at the end of the block so we had total southern exposure as well as windows facing east and west. Unlike the other houses on the side street, attached on both sides, we had the long side of the house facing out with windows from one end to the other, The place was, therefore, light and airy and always clean and freshly painted. Yet, no one on TV in the 50s lived in places like that. If they didn't live on a farm or a ranch, they lived in houses. These houses were large, always had an upstairs, a dining room where the whole family would eat breakfast together on a weekday, and were surrounded by grass for the boys to cut as part of their assigned chores. Of course, no TV town named Springfield was populated by Italian widows in black dresses who barely spoke English.

As a child, I thought anyone older than my parents was ancient. Later, I learned that many of these women were only in their late 50s and early 60s. Their lives were so hard and so lacking in joy that they were old most of their lives. Often in mourning black dresses since someone was always recently buried, I associated sad dull lives with being Italian. The neighborhood was filled with women like this, often sitting in front of their houses in folding chairs, watching our small corner of the world go by around them.

"Pascalina's husband was killed in World War I," Mother explained. "He lived here but went back to fight for Italy. He said it was his duty. He was killed by a shell on the way to the front. That poor woman raised her daughter all alone." I had no sense of economics then, of course, but I knew that Pascalina derived some income from her crocheting skills. We lived above my uncle's chrome furniture store, of which there will be much to say. Part of his inventory was doilies, and dolls with dresses she created. I guess the few dollars she made from her handiwork helped a bit. Looking back, I can't imagine what kind of money that brought in but, after all, it was an era of five-cent candy bars, fifteen-cent hot dogs, and pushcarts of eight-cent knishes. A hundred dollars a week was a big salary.

"Don't look at the cripple," Pascalina said. "It bring you bad luck." There was a sad looking old man on our block who walked slowly with a cane and had a severe limp. "Hello, *giovanotto*," he would say in heavily accented English. The man was friendly enough but Pascalina's warnings frightened me. These were not the people I saw on TV. Why did I live in a place so different from the rest of America?

"Pascalina is very superstitious," Mother explained. "You don't get bad luck for looking at an old man who doesn't walk so good. If he says hello to you, you say hello back. It is important to be polite to people. You want people to think you're a good boy."

One day, I was around the corner on the short block between two larger streets, Fermi Place. There wasn't much through traffic so the City designated it a play street. I must have dressed myself that day since my polo shirt was inside out. One of the mothers pointed that out to me and said, "Commere, Brian, I'll fix it for ya." Pascalina was sitting nearby and intervened, "Nooo...It bad luck to change. You gotta wear it like that till you take it off later."

Chapter 2. The Hood

My neighborhood didn't have a name. Sometimes we said Brownsville, but that was several blocks to the south. Sometimes, East New York, but that was several blocks to the southeast. We never said Bedford Stuyvesant even though it was the same distance from our enclave as the other areas we would name. Bed Stuy was populated by African Americans, or to use the polite term then in use, "coloreds." Only bleeding heart liberals, of whom there were none in my immediate vicinity, said "Negro."

Brooklyn has a long and complex history. It started in colonial times as farmland, punctuated by villages and hills. It was the site of the first battle fought by the Continental Army during the Revolutionary War. The population grew as docks were built and Brooklyn became a major port. Eventually, as the population of New York City grew, Brooklyn grew as well and the villages and farmlands were consolidated into the City of Brooklyn. As its own city, it had a City Hall, and a baseball team. Prospect Park was designed by the same men who designed Central Park on the island of Manhattan. A short distance from my block but seemingly a world away was Grand Army Plaza, the gateway to Prospect Park. The Plaza was a large circle created by Flatbush Avenue and several cross streets. The Plaza has a Civil War memorial arch with bronze statutes of military men on the top and on the side, larger and more magnificent than anything in Manhattan. There is a downtown, known in the past for its restaurants and theaters, now a business and technology hub.

In 1898, Brooklyn, Manhattan, the Bronx, Queens County and Staten Island were consolidated into Greater New York, the City as it exists today. By 1930 Brooklyn was the most populous of the New York City boroughs and remains so today.

There are volumes of books written about Brooklyn, its history, culture, and people. Coney Island was a unique amusement area, with Steeple Chase and Luna Park, the Cyclone, the Wonder Wheel, Nathan's hot dogs, and a mile of crowded beach. Flatbush was the home of the Brooklyn Dodgers at Ebbets Field. Brownsville was a heavily Jewish area, filled with retail such as Fortunoff's, eateries like Kishka King, and the ornate movie palace, the Lowe's Pitkin. Downtown Brooklyn had the Brooklyn Paramount and the Fox theaters, Junior's restaurant, and Macy's and A&S department stores. Ocean Parkway that led to Coney Island was considered an upscale destination for Jewish families. In contrast to the popular image of Brooklyn as the home of Ralph Kramden, Brooklyn Heights, with its tree-lined streets and brownstones, was populated by the borough's WASP establishment.

After my family left for greener pastures, community school districts were created. The schools were consolidated into the Ocean Hill Brownsville district so, finally, my former turf had a name that we didn't use when I lived there.

This was, and still is, a part of Brooklyn that doesn't make it into the Brooklyn literature of nostalgia, the books about how quaint life was back then, in the simpler era, when a nickel could buy a candy bar or a pack of baseball cards, a long pretzel rod was two cents, and everyone was a Dodgers fan. This was not brownstone Brooklyn, nor one of the areas with large private houses. My neighborhood was dominated by five-story apartment buildings and two and three-story wood frame shingle houses with railroad rooms, one room leading to another with no doors to afford privacy. My house and all the others on the block were built in 1899. If there was a "modern" bathroom, it was added later. Ours had the toilet tank on the wall so gravity let the water down to flush the bowl, like the one where the gun was hidden in the restaurant in *The Godfather* when Michael Corleone killed the corrupt police captain and the mobster he was protecting. Cousin Vito's two-story house only had a bathtub on the upper floor so Aunt Lucy's cousin, who lived downstairs, came up for a bath every Friday night. Bathing was at best a weekly ritual then.

My immediate area was dominated by the House of the Good Samaritan, which everyone called "Good Sam." Built before the houses in the neighborhood, this was a nineteenth century Catholic fortress run by nuns to house girls in "trouble." Directly across Atlantic Avenue from my house, all our windows faced this edifice. The property stretched four city blocks in one direction and two blocks in the other, with one street running between the walled-in gardens and the actual buildings. The entire place was surrounded by a high brick wall with broken glass embedded on the top. The main building was five stories topped with a cupola. The place had the look of a prison which, in fact, it was.

As a young boy, I was told it was a home for girls. At the time, that was enough for me. One day, however, there were police cars at Good Sam. I was told that a girl escaped. Even at my young age, I realized that this was more than a home, it was a jail.

My mother told me that bad girls were sent there. I later learned that civil judges or parents sentenced girls to the care of the nuns for such crimes as staying out late or hanging out with the wrong people. "Those girls are American or Irish," according to my mother. "Italians take care of their families."

One afternoon, I was bouncing a rubber ball against the garage doors of our house. Mother was sitting on a beach chair and Jessica was in a stroller. It was a typical late afternoon on Atlantic Avenue. The kids were home from school, mothers were sitting on the stoops, not yet in the kitchens making dinner, and there were many passers by on this main thoroughfare. A woman who seemed to be my mother's age stopped, looked at my mother and said "Millie Mazzola? I ain't seen you since Lane." Mother seemed a bit embarrassed and hesitated before she answered. "My God, Norma, it has been about 15 years. What happened to you?" "What didn't happen to me," was her reply. "If you have time," Mother said, "wanna come upstairs for a cup of tea?"

I went upstairs too and retreated to my room. Since our apartment was small, the railroad layout allowed me to hear a conversation in other rooms. I was told I had "big ears" which was a gentle put down for a kid who heard and remembered a conversation. Mother served tea in the living room which was separated from my room by my parent's bedroom so I listened to their entire conversation.

After the preliminary conversation starters about how Mom married Peter and how many children she has and a bit about her brothers and sister, it was Norma's turn.

"When I was a junior in Lane, I started going out with Tommy Verasco. Remember him? One night, he borrowed his brother's car and we drove out to Canarsie, and parked near the water. We were, ya know, kissin and stuff and a cop car stopped next to us. They brought us to the police station and called my parents. The cops said we could be charged with indecent exposure. The next day, this judge said he would drop the charges if my mother and father agreed to send me to Good Sam, ya know, right across the street. Millie, I was there until I was twenty one. That's why I didn't graduate with you."

"I lived across the street all my life," mother interjected, "but I have no idea what it's like inside."

"God, it was awful. We had no protection. The nuns ran everything. There was no place to complain about how we were treated. We had no idea what was going on in the world. No radio, no newspapers. We didn't know if we were winning or losing the war. A whole bunch of us slept in a big room, on flat mattresses with a thin blanket. We were always cold in the winter and hot in the summer.

There was no soap, no toothpaste or underwear unless someone brought it for you. My mother came with stuff once in awhile but my father never came. He was too ashamed. And we were only allowed one visitor a month. I could write only two letters a month and the nuns read everything that came in or out. I could never write about how bad the place was, so I only used my letters to ask for stuff I needed. Of course, no candy or makeup or comic books were allowed only soap and stuff like that."

"The damn nuns even made money off the work we did. We did some sewing for who knows who. We found out the nuns were getting paid for our work but we didn't get nothin."

"Let me tell ya, Millie, they really messed up my life. I never graduated high school, Tommy got drafted and I never heard from him again. His cousin told me he married some girl from New Jersey that he met when he was stationed at Fort Dix. Who knows? So I got married to a jerk who left me and I have had shitty factory jobs since I got out. Remember how we studied business in school? I really wanted to be a secretary in some nice office in New York. Never happened."

I took in every word. I finally understood what that fortress that dominated our neighborhood was all about. I didn't know what "indecent exposure" meant but I didn't think that a girl should go to jail for sitting in a car with her boyfriend. Not in America, at least.

"Why do they call him, Pasqual?," Mother said. "Why don't they call him Pat?" Pasqual was a boy about my age, who had recently come from Italy. He wasn't in the country long enough to Americanize his name, but, like her own name, she preferred names that did not sound Italian. The neighborhood was a mix of Italian American, Jewish, African American and a smattering of the Germans who were earlier settlers. Even in a mixed neighborhood, blocks tended to be, but not exclusively, populated by one group. The Italian Americans were mostly second and third generation, grandparents born in Italy, but parents and children born in the U.S.A.

This pattern was broken with great force when a family from Italy moved in to the house next door.

One afternoon, there was a great deal of commotion next door. Our garage and hence our garage roof, touched that house, so there were no neighbors closer. Suitcases, trunks, boxes, and furniture, along with what seemed to be an endless stream of people of all ages, especially children, were entering and exiting the house and spilling into the street. The youngest boys were running all over the sidewalk and into the heavily trafficked Atlantic Avenue, ignoring the cars and trucks and causing a cacophony of horns and screeches as drivers tried to avoid the boys who seemed to have no sense of an urban neighborhood.

We learned that this family came from a small village well outside Naples but we never knew what they did once they reached our turf. There was a father who was always red faced from wine, a mother who dressed like a peasant from years passed, and numerous children, ranging from about five to mid teens. Rosie was my age, hard and tough, but was somewhat rational when not angry. She hung out with the kids on the block but I knew I had to be careful what I said and did around her because of her quick temper. Several of the children were mentally challenged with difficulty expressing themselves except by hitting. Jessica was terrified by Ralphie, a boy her age, who wanted to play with her but didn't know how. When she played in front of the house, I was sure to be around to protect her from Ralphie whose behavior was inconsistent at best, but mostly irrational.

One day, the street in front of our house was full of police cars and an ambulance. Ralphie was struck by a city bus as he ran out into the street. He disappeared for a few weeks in a hospital which clearly lowered the stress level for Jessica, or anyone else who was horrified by his dangerous behavior of darting in and out of a main thoroughfare. Apparently, his mother prayed to Saint Anthony for his recovery.

When he came home from the hospital, he was clad in a brown monk's robe, tied by a rope, wearing sandals, the way the Saint was depicted in statues and paintings. The outfit did not last long. First, the robe disappeared, leaving him with a brown tee shirt and shorts, then, eventually, he went back to normal clothes having lost or destroyed his devotional attire.

Years later, when Mother and I were talking about the old neighborhood, I brought up Ralphie and Saint Anthony. She denied this happened. I said that this was something I could not make up but she refused to admit that Italians, even admittedly a family that stood out as these did, could have done something so primitive and superstitious. Yet, she did remember her encounters with Maria, the teenage daughter.

Maria was about 16 or so with dark hair and big eyes. She looked like an actress from Italian movies although I was too young to have any interest in her. She was the age of my teenage cousins. I had no sexual urges at that age, of course. My crushes were on whatever cute girl my age was around, or the distant figures on TV like Sky King's niece Penny or Annette from the Mickey Mouse Club. The TV girls were abstract fantasy figures, not real or personal, and certainly in no way of a sexual interest, not at that age at least. Maria never spoke to me so there was never a big sister/cousin/neighbor connection.

She came to the house and had talks with my mother, about which I paid no attention, even if I overheard. They were mostly in Italian anyway but I could see that mother treated her with kindness as if she needed a sane older woman in her life which her family certainly did not provide. I do remember her trying on a dressy dress of my mother's although I had no idea why or what occasion was upcoming. In short, Maria was a neighbor who played absolutely no part in my experiences.

Decades later, when the subject of that family came up, long after we left the old turf, and she figured that at thirty five or so, I was old enough to handle it, my mother told me that one night a week was for

Maria's father. Along with the violence, drunkenness, and mental illness of that family, there was also incest. Throw in the adultery since the father's "gummare" also visited, there was a full picture of a family that was nothing like I had known through several generations of Italian Americans. Yet, the Saint Anthony story was too embarrassing for mother to bear?

From our perch one level above the street our garage roof penthouse afforded a view above the fray. We could observe without being close enough to participate. We certainly did not want to be close enough to Vincent who we called "Vigenze" who was about 12 or 13, with broad shoulders and an ape like manner. Like other members of the family, he had a mental handicap of some sort. He would climb the large tree directly across Atlantic Avenue and let out cries like Tarzan. He threatened to kill me a few times for minor offenses I have long forgotten but he himself would never be.

Mother was embarrassed when we had guests. "Everybody has to see who lives next door to us? I am so ashamed that they are Italians." My reply was predicable, I guess. "Why does it matter that they are Italian? We are American."

Our neighborhood was not known for producing scholars but organized crime was firmly rooted there. Mother, quite casually, talked about the family that rented the third floor apartment many years before I was born. "They were part of Murder Incorporated," she said. Murder Incorporated was a gang of diverse killers, both Italian and Jewish, who killed for hire in the 30s and 40s until District Attorney Thomas Dewey prosecuted them and sent several to the electric chair. It was a neighborhood story that my father told that when Happy Maione was executed someone sent his mother flowers in the form of the electric chair.

"One night Uncle Mike was driven home by his friend and they sat in the car talking for awhile before he came up," Mother said. "The man upstairs said 'Mikey, when you come home, you gotta get out of the car fast. I almost shot you.' Imagine living like that always looking out the window to see if someone is going to kill you?" "It musta been a bad neighborhood then with all those gangsters," I presumed. "Nah, they didn't bother you on the street, not like the coloreds today," she explained.

The older boys talked about the Fulton and Rockaways, a local gang, mostly Italian. As I kid I didn't come into much contact with gangs so I really didn't know what they actually did. I did learn later, that John Gotti, "the dapper don" did his internship with this group. Since he rose to the top of the local mobster elite, I could only assume the training provided was effective. I was never tempted to associate with them, even though an early start would provide seniority later on. My vision was outside the neighborhood that I desperately wanted to leave.

Frankie and Anthony, two of the older boys, took the gang thing very seriously. They were not members but I had the feeling that they wanted to be. They were torn, though, since they weren't thugs so would not provide the muscle, or do anything really bad. Yet, they admired how the Fulton and Rockaways stuck together, and were treated with respect. "Nobody messes with them," Anthony said. "Yeah, and they keep the niggers out of the neighborhood." Frankie added. "The whole block around the corner are coloreds," I replied. Frankie then explained that they stayed on one block. Brooklyn, obviously, had its tribal borders.

As a working class area, there were no bookstores. There didn't seem to be people who read books. Atlantic Avenue, however, was a center of the used tire industry. On summer mornings when I didn't have to get up early for school, I would be awakened by the clang of sledge hammers removing tires from the rims at Tony's tire store across narrow Fermi Place right outside my window. This was one of several and the owners all seemed to be named Tony. They would regroove the tires with a tool that cut small strips of rubber from the tires. These strips were all over the streets and sometimes served when we made sling shots if we could find the right shaped piece of wood that may have fallen off a tree. This was not a usual occurrence but in an era with little access to weaponry, any thing would do. The older boys would make carpet guns that used a heavy rubber band or the tire remnants to project a piece of linoleum. I had not seen one used in actual combat but the boys often talked about their arsenals just in case there was intrusion from other races or even from Italians from another block.

There were always kids on Fermi Place since it was only one block long and designated a "Play Street." And play we did. Aside from punch ball and stoop ball, there was hide and seek. The words "hide and go seek" were contracted to "hanglo seek" then just "hanglo." There was a game that involved pushing bottle caps, called "checkers" to various places marked on the asphalt with chalk. This game was called "skelly" also known on the block as "scully." There was probably no official name since it was a made up street game with no tournaments or organizations.

The language the boys used was colorful even at an early age. There was no profanity in my house so I wasn't aware of the "f word" so I heard the compound word beginning with "mother" as "mother jumper" or "mother Fletcher." I never used "curse" words since that was also on the list of venial sins that had to be confessed.

The guys in the neighborhood used the English language in strange ways. A boy living in the house on the corner was new to the block. He was from New Orleans and his mother was considering moving back to her family's house where she grew up and was Mother's best friend. His name was Albert. Someone mentioned the town in New Mexico so he became Albert Turkey, then eventually just "Turkey."

Morphing Albuquerque into "Albert Turkey" was an example of a word I didn't know at the time but became one of my favorites later-- banal. Even as a young boy, I was unimpressed by the simplistic comments and obviousness of things people said. "Brian, you're short." Wow, how did they come up with that one? When I lost my baby teeth and before the others grew in, I cannot count the number of times I heard someone sing "All I want for Christmas is my two front teeth..." a popular song at the time.

The people upstairs had a boy a few years older than me so he was one of the big kids who looked after me, watching their language, and being careful when discussing the breasts of their contemporary neighborhood girls. His parents came from Italy in the 1930s but could not bring his brother Joe since Mussolini did not let military age males leave the country. Joe married and had a son who we called "Little Anthony" to distinguish him from his uncle, upstairs, also named Anthony. They eventually came to the country and were welcomed at a small party upstairs. Little Anthony spoke no English at first but learned by hanging out with his uncle and the rest of the boys. Of course, learning that way meant his first words and expressions were street slang. "Get outta here," and "The niggers betta not come on this block," were a few phrases I recall.

The racial divide was real as more African Americans moved in to adjacent areas. "I never go past Saratoga Avenue because of the coloreds," or "Don't go past Fulton Street," and similar phrases were frequently heard. Not that anyone needed convincing of the danger we were facing but one incident validated what everyone was thinking.

In my elementary school, we had school bank days where we brought in small amounts of money and our bankbooks to be collected and deposited in the East New York Savings Bank. One of such days, while entering a rear door of the school, carrying my banking envelope, I was jumped by three older boys who took the money. I wasn't hurt but clearly frightened. I reported the mugging to school authorities who called my mother. An older teacher who acted as some sort of dean tried to get me to say that this happened outside the school. As a totally honest kid, I had no idea that she was trying to keep the school out of it. No, I insisted, I was jumped IN the school.

Weeks later, my parents got a call for us to go to a local court. My father had to take a day off and kept saying "I'm not a crusader." I had no idea what he meant. The only association I had with the word "crusader" was a cartoon character on TV "Crusader Rabbit." We did go to the court and were met by a detective who said that they caught the colored boys who took your money. According to my father, the detective was Italian. I remember him saying that if anything else happened to me, he will break some heads. I was led into the courtroom, empty except for the judge and the three boys. I stood in the back and heard the judge say "You don't go to bed when you want. You go to bed when they tell you. You don't eat what you want, you eat what they give you." Obviously, they were being sent to some sort of juvenile detention facility. Looking back, all this was for a gain of $1.25. I have always wondered if they were rehabilitated.

Even though I was a constant reader with a head full of facts about history, baseball, and military stuff, there wasn't much talk of those things on the block. Always trying to be a regular guy to avoid being picked on, which, fortunately, I was not, I did partake of the street culture. Comic books were popular, as was punch ball, roller skates, and the local cuisine. The latter consisted on fifteen cent hot dogs from the cart across the street, eight cent knishes from a roving cart, later raised to 10 cents, and egg creams. Egg creams were a Brooklyn invention. They had no eggs and no cream. They were made with a small amount of milk, chocolate syrup, and seltzer. Somehow, these ingredients worked together to create a product unique to New York City, and one that was firmly ensconced in Brooklyn nostalgia lore.

Chapter 3. The Big Brother

"Daddy, what's the name of that song?" "Kiss of Fire."

    I usually woke up before my mother and went to the kitchen where my father would be drinking coffee and smoking a cigarette before he left for work. He listened to his portable radio, a large RCA metal thing which must have been state of the art before transistors. I remember the songs his station played at the time, pop music in the period between the big bands and rock and roll. "If I give my heart to you, will you handle it with care?" So sang Denise Lor.

    "Jambalaya and a crawfish pie and fillet gumbo

    Cause tonight I'm gonna see my cher amio

    Pick guitar fill fruit jar and be gay-o

    Son of a gun we'll have big fun on the bayou"

    "Daddy, I don't understand those words." "That is a song from New Orleans," Peter replied. "They speak Creole down there. That part of the country used to be French so they have a different language. Mommy and me went there for our honeymoon and we couldn't understand some of the people."

    I later learned that song was written and performed by Hank Williams, but the version on New York radio was sung by Jo Stafford, a 50s chanteuse. In the mist of memory, the input in my early life was mellow, middle of the road, and easy to take. And the music was a reflection of the same. Perry Como, Dean Martin, and children's records were heard in the house. There was no classical, jazz, R&B, or folk music. The warm sounds of early morning radio were also part of a warm life of comfort, care and love. Aside from Poison Zoomack, nothing scary entered my insular, protected life. Except the nightmares.

"Where do you live," my father would ask. "Twenny sixty three alantagavenue," I would reply. "What is your telephone number?" "Hyacinth five, two four three six," was my practiced reply. All this was in case I got lost. Since, at the age of three, I was never alone, there wasn't much chance of that but the possibility of getting lost, being away from my parents or a close relative, was real to me, or why else would I have to memorize all that data?

The recurring dream took place in front of our house. It was dark. Even though we lived on a main thoroughfare, it was quiet. There were no cars. The only people were a few feet away from me. My father, with his back to me, was talking to three or four men his age. The scene was like a de Chirico painting, buildings, and shadows, devoid of movement. Rising above the apartment buildings across the avenue and a block away, larger than twenty moons, was a woman's face. It was not one that I knew. Nor was it the face of a monster. But it should not have been there. The few people around my father didn't notice anything and there was no one else around to view this phenomenon. I called to my father but no words came out. All I needed to do was to get his attention and I would be safe. But he couldn't hear me because I had no voice.

Another recurring dream was where I floated out of my bed, past my sleeping parents in the adjoining bedroom, through the living room and dining room of our railroad apartment. I woke up as I got to the kitchen about to float out the window. Nothing happened that was particularly frightening, yet I felt a sense of dread. Suppose I floated out the window, into the dark night sky, never to see my parents again? In these dreams, I had no power or control. I could not speak in order to get anyone's attention. I could not move beyond the floating. In the dream in front of the house, I could not walk over to the safety of my father. In my dreams, I had no power to respond, to flee, to call for help. I was a helpless victim.

In my dream, the store on the ground level of my house was closed as was everything else nearby. In real life, it was an active, busy place that was a neighborhood hangout. Uncle Louie ran a business that sold Formica kitchen and dinette sets. Dinette sets were small tables with a small matching china cabinet for the apartments that didn't have a full dining room, which was just about all the dwellings in the area. The seats were of vinyl or "leatherette," plastic made to look somewhat like leather, with chrome frames. In fact, the store was called Atlantic Chrome.

A large part of the business was the reupholstering of the chairs as wear and tare caused the vinyl to spilt, so the attached two-car garage was converted into a shop with equipment to stretch and hold the materials, including padding such as foam rubber. Uncle Louie hired and trained some of the local young men to do this work and they became part of the crowd that I saw every day.

"Louie hires niggers now?," Aunt Rose said as we pulled up in her husband's car one weekday. "I hate niggers. They have such white teeth." Uncle Louie did not feel the same way as the boys reflected the neighborhood. One was Puerto Rican, another African American, another Italian.

Uncle Louie lived just across Atlantic Avenue from the store so his wife, Aunt Rhoda, and his daughters, Marie and Loretta, were always around, either in or in front of the store, or visiting Mother on the second floor. Another uncle, Mike, was a letter carrier and usually came around after he finished his route by early afternoon.

Mike took his job with the Post Office quite seriously. He treated his uniform with the gravity due the accoutrements of the military. The patent leather brim of this hat was shined to a mirror-like gloss. The brass buttons of his jacket were polished periodically and his shoes were spit shined. In those days, working for the United States government was considered to be an honor, long before "going postal" was shorthand for insanely violent behavior.

Uncle Mike liked tea in the afternoon. He preferred it in a glass which was how Mother prepared it for him. With one brother in the store downstairs, one drinking tea in her kitchen, and the other living two blocks away, Millie was surrounded by her older brothers, not much different from when she was growing up in that same house. When together, they seemed to have so much to talk about, even though they were always together. They talked about Momma and Papa and relatives with names I was familiar with but did not know. When Mike's son Vito was born, Millie told me that he will not be around so much now that he had a boy of this own. Of course, since Mike and his wife Francesca, "Aunt Fran," only lived four blocks away, and Fran's aunt lived two houses away from us, we saw plenty of all of them.

Years later, long after Uncle Mike died of cancer at 62, I was sitting with Mother at her suburban home. My children were splashing around in the kid's pool my father set up when his grandchildren visited. She and I were chatting about things from the past, present and future. Just then, an African American postal worker, in shorts, delivered Mother's mail. "Remember how Uncle Mike used to be so proud that he worked for the government and wore that uniform?" I nodded in assent. "What would he think," she asked, "if he saw a colored woman, in shorts no less, delivering the mail?"

One afternoon, when I was three, sitting in the kitchen with Mother and my father, Peter, he said "We are going to have a baby. You are going to be a big brother. We need you to help Mommy and Daddy take care of the baby." Wow, I thought, I was going to be promoted to Big Brother. I knew this was an awesome responsibility but I knew I was up to the task. Why not? I was not yet in school, I was always surrounded by loved ones, and didn't yet mix with kids on the street.

Because of this cocoon of home and family, I had not yet been challenged. Therefore, I had never failed. So, of course, I knew I would be good as a big brother, whatever that job was to be.

As the center of attention of my own life, I don't remember Mother's pregnancy. If she had morning sickness, or any discomfort, I wasn't aware of it. She didn't say anything to me and I never heard her say anything to anyone else. All I knew was that she was busy cooking, cleaning, doing the wash, hanging the wash on the clothesline, ironing and taking care of her father. Sure, I noticed that her belly was growing. She told me that was a sign from God that a baby was coming. When I asked where babies came from, I was told "from heaven." While I usually took what I heard from adults at face value, I thought this explanation needed more detail. "Does the baby come down slow, from the sky?" "No, Brian, the baby appears one day in the hospital."

When the day finally came, my father told me that I had a baby sister whose name is Jessica. From that point on, I knew that my job was to help to take care of the baby. I wasn't sure what that really meant but I was going to be the big brother that meant a lot to me. I went with my father to pick up mom and Jessica and was really excited that there was a baby in the house. I didn't know that half the neighborhood was going to be there when we brought the baby home. There were the usual "ooo's" and "ahhh's" and "Godda bless," since a number of the visitors where not native English speakers. What really pissed me off, however, was that some of these people were actually touching my baby! I remember the big hands on some of the women reaching out to lift Jessica. This was all wrong. Only mommy and daddy and I could touch the baby. I wished they would all leave so I could talk to Jessica and explain that I was her big brother and here to protect her.

Despite Mother's middle class, modern American aspirations, she bought in to many of the superstitions traditional to the villages in Italy from where our ancestors originated. Jessica was running a fever that wouldn't break. I later learned that my mother feared polio. However, there was always the possibility that the baby's condition was caused by "mal occhio," the evil eye. Fortunately, there was an antidote. She put oil in a little bowl and dipped her finger, then held her finger over a plate of water, so that the oil fell in droplets. If the oil stayed in a small drop, the evil eye was not around. If, however, the drop spread quickly over the plate of water, the evil eye was present. This was accompanied by the sign of the cross and various prayers. Of course, she did not explain all this to me, nor did I learn the results, probably because at five, I was too young to understand the mysteries. She cried with joy when Doctor Martino told her that Jessica had the measles.

I was not trained in the arts of Italian rituals of this nature so I did my job of protecting Jessica in American ways. I went to her crib every morning and talked to her. I watched my mother bathe and change her. I was thrilled when she began to know who I was and smile at me. I made sure she had access to her toys and I read her stories when she was old enough to understand words. In the 1950s, there were serious baby carriages, designed to withstand land mines. Millie would leave the carriage under a tree in front of the house and ask me to watch her. I was no more than 5 at the time but no one saw anything wrong, dangerous, or worthy of reporting if a mother left a baby on the sidewalk in the custody of a five-year old. This was only a few feet from my uncle's chrome store, a major center of activity and, looking back, my world, or at least that part of it, felt very safe.

"It's an American plane," I argued. When the extended families on both sides were full of kids, there were birthday parties almost once a month. These were in the house and included the grownups. There were no bowling, ice skating, or gymnastics parties then. No venues especially for kids. The small apartments and houses were filled wall to wall with kids and parents. Kids formed alliances based on age and sex. God forbid if a "little kid" tried to breach the phalanx of the guys my age. Being nice or "nurturing" was out of the question then. Societal norms had to be respected. Except for one very much older cousin, cousins Vito from my mother's side and Michael from my father's side, and me, were the oldest male cousins. There was no greater thrill than to have both of these lads together, where they helped to form a barrier against intrusion from some inappropriate upstart. We never had to worry about the girls trying to move in, but there were some boys as much as a year and a half younger than us who dared to attempt to hang with us. We would never let that happen.

There were presents at these parties, of course. We dreaded clothes but only the oldest aunts, whose own kids were grown, would be lame enough to think clothes were an appropriate gift for a young boy. For my fourth birthday, someone gave me a large metal passenger plane. The plane had a decal of the American flag and the words "Pan American." When I told cousin Loretta that this was an American plane, her response was "It is a Pan American plane." I insisted that it was an AMERICAN plane but she would not back off. I shouted "It's made by Pan American but it's an AMERICAN plane." Of course, at that age, I did not know the relationship between a company and a nation but my fervent patriotism caused me to favor anything that was "American."

In our neighborhood and family, there was no question that the United States was the greatest country in the world. Even when my horizon expanded to my school, there was no social commentary, not even on the lowest level. World War II was not even over for ten years and my father and my uncles served in the military as did just about all the men of military age. They returned from a great victory, proud of their service and only seeing a bright future ahead. Since I was not yet in school with the American flag in every room, and each day beginning with the Pledge of Allegiance, there were no outside forces telling me how great America was. But it was the constant talk from my father, mother, aunts and uncles. The war was over, the Great Depression had passed and the United States was perfect. There was no hand wringing over the plight of the Indians, for example. They were only the people that we saw in movies and TV attacking the cavalry, or as we said "calvary." Movies did not deal with the nuances of why there were Indian wars. Sure, Cochise was a good guy and Tonto was a great sidekick for the Lone Ranger but, basically, Indians were a threat to those pioneers rightfully settling the West. And we knew nothing about how the Texas Rangers terrorized and oppressed the Mexican population.

Eisenhower was president and, therefore, a respected grandfatherly figure. I was outraged that Adlai Stevenson would actually run against him. The president was America, how could anyone vote against him? I was greatly relieved when Adlai was soundly beaten.

There was never any discussion about the plight of African Americans, or "coloreds" as we called them. I did not know that schools in the South were segregated or that there were restaurants, theaters, water fountains, and transportation facilities for white and black people. The discussion about them was about how they were ruining one neighborhood after another in Brooklyn, causing white people to move to the suburbs. Italians had a code word for them, which was a mispronunciation of the Italian word for eggplant. They called them "mulenyam." Even when there was an African-American with undeniable talent, my parents would put a negative spin on them. Willie Mays was a good ballplayer but he was a show off. Nat King Cole sang well but was ugly. Lena Horne had a big mouth. When watching a traveling basketball team show their stuff on TV, my father referred to them as the "Globetrotters." It was years later when I first heard their full name, "the Harlem Globetrotters."

Once, while discussing why people go to the Caribbean, Millie said "If I want to see coloreds, I'll stay in Brooklyn." She was also very particular about who I took things from or whose house I visited. I had to ask first. On one occasion, an African-American friend from around the corner offered me a piece of gum. I ran upstairs to ask and was told no.

One day when my father took a day off from work for some reason, he took Jessica to school. When the kids lined up with their partners before entering, he saw that Jessica was holding hands with a black boy, another first grader. He went home and told m mother about it. He was so outraged that he was now determined to move. He told that story many times in later years as if it were something to be proud of.

We didn't know or didn't care about social problems. TV and movies led us to believe that America was a country of respectable white people like the family on "Father Knows Best." There was nothing to criticize about America, except, perhaps those who criticized America.

That patriotism was part of the curriculum of the school that was on the horizon as the next rite of passage of my life.

Chapter 4. The Scholar and Patriot

"It's only two weeks," my mother said to the woman seated at a table in the hallway. Little did I know what that meant or that it would impact my life.

"We are going to school to register so you could go to kindergarden," Mother said. We walked the two blocks to the same school that she attended. It was a red stone Victorian structure that was warm inside and painted with institutional blue and white. There was a basement with a lunch room and toilets, three floors of classrooms and the auditorium that took up the entire fourth floor. The desks were metal, bolted in place to the floor and topped with varnished wood that still had holes for the inkwells used by past generations of kids.

At registration, I did not get beyond the hallway nor did I envision what was to come.

The "two weeks" mentioned by my mother was the period of time after the deadline that my birthday occurred. The cut off was December 1 and my birthday was in mid December. Somehow, however, she beat the bureaucracy and I was registered, thus beginning my career as the youngest in the class.

Finally, the big day came. The first day of school. For the first day, we had to look nice although the family creed was to always look presentable so no one would talk about you, which meant that no one would talk about our mothers. In the days before global warming, September mornings were cool. The small schoolyard was full of kids and the kindergarten teachers led us into the classroom. Joined by my best friend, cousin Vito, we marched into the room. It was a large corner classroom with movable tables and chairs, large windows, and shelves with books, papers, a toy kitchen, and the various accoutrements of education in an era when kindergarten was the first school experience and the first time away from our mothers. There was the choice of either the morning or afternoon session. My mother selected the shorter two hour afternoon. With a young baby, it was probably easier to get me to school at one o'clock than at nine.

That first day, I learned that gender mattered. The teacher took us to the basement to the toilets. "Go tend to yourself," the elderly teacher said. I had no idea what that meant. She must have pointed the girls to the left since they went skipping off to the girls' room. I thought they were going to get lost since they were going in the opposite direction from the boys. If memory serves, we didn't lose any girls that day.

The two hours lasted forever, but the day ended and mom was there to pick me up. I felt like a big kid now that I was at school but it then dawned on me that I would have to go back the next day to begin a life sentence.

For reasons that I did not understand then, and maybe still don't, I cried and protested as my mother brought me to school the second day. I clearly did not want to be separated from my mother, having never experienced separation before. The school was pleasant enough. The teacher, Miss Forester, was kind. My classmates were nice kids and I even had my cousin Vito with me. I handled the tasks easily and even made some observations and comments that led me to be known as the smartest boy in the class. One time, the teacher lit a candle in a jar, covered the jar, and extinguished the flame. "Why did the candle go out?" she asked. Using the best scientific method of observation, hypothesis, and conclusion, I politely raised my hand. "The fire needs air," I said. "Yes. Brian. A fire cannot burn without air." Wow. I figured that out, was brave enough to share my theory, was recognized as the boy who knows stuff by the teacher, and began earning the respect of my classmates. This, after all, was not a bad gig, but still, two hours away from my mother was just too long.

The school was a reflection of the neighborhood. It was on the cusp of Brownsville, East New York, and Bed Stuy and the student body was a mix of Jewish, Italian, African American and Hispanic, the latter were lumped together as "Portaricans." As little kids, race and religion didn't mean much until constant comments and reminders from adults made us aware of differences. "Portaricans jab with knives, coloreds only slash," I heard my father say. "Don't take candy from coloreds," Mother would say.

One day, I picked up the phone. The voice on the line asked to speak to my father. I could tell that the caller was African American and knew that several of my father's co-workers fit that description. "Daddy, your colored friend is calling." The house filled with shusses as I handed the phone to my father. Frank Smith came to the house later that day. Knowing how everyone in the family felt about people of color, I don't know why my father invited him over. The visit was uneventful. The guest had some alcoholic beverage and left. My mother took the glass and said that it should be sterilized.

As we approached the all-important Christmas season, an episode of "Walt Disney's Disneyland" aired on a Sunday evening. My life now had a new focus.

The episode was "Davy Crockett Indian Fighter." Fess Parker played the legendary American character. He was the bravest, strongest, most upstanding character I had ever known. He fought under Andrew Jackson in the Creek war during the War of 1812. He never missed a shot, or lost at hand to hand combat. He knew the ways of the woods and how to fight Indians. When the pompous regular Major Norton ordered his men to fire a volley at the charging Creeks, they ducked and escaped through the army lines as the solders reloaded. My father explained that in those days, the rifles had to be reloaded with shot and powder after each shot. That was my first history lesson.

The second episode that aired a few weeks later showed Davy as a politician and ultimately a member of the House of Representatives from Tennessee. There were no battles in that episode and Davy shed his buckskins for clothes appropriate to Congress. He stood up for what was right. He opposed then President Jackson's bill to move all Native Americans, which we called Indians, west of the Mississippi. This caused him to lose his seat.

Davy Crockett was a huge marketing success for Disney. I had the outfit, complete with coonskin hat, plus the genuine licensed rifle. I was a stickler for accuracy and hated when any of the boys borrowed my rifle and shot, cocked the hammer and fired again. I protested that the rifle had to be powdered, the ball inserted, then the whole thing had to be rammed in, before the gun could fire. I absolutely hated when the guys would not play by my rules since the rules were based on historical fact.

Every item imaginable came out with a Davy Crockett image-- lunch boxes, toy knives, and trading cards. Of course, I had the whole set of cards, purchased in packages of five or six along with a flat piece of pink chewing gun. They seemed to have one for every frame of the series. Later on, just like my baseball cards, my mother felt free to discard them without asking me if I wanted to keep them.

The TV episodes were strung together as a full-length movie. Of course, my father took me to see it. This time, in color, when TVs at home were black and white on a small screen. For months, whenever we drove past a patch of woods, usually the side of Long Island parkways, I thought that was the perfect spot for a home movie of me in my Davy Crockett get up. It was a concept that never reached the production stage.

When it was time for the final episode of the Crockett trilogy, my father gave me a warning that I didn't want to believe. Davy, along with his trusted fictional sidekick Georgie Russell, was on a riverboat going down the Mississippi. They met a gambler dressed in fancy duds named Thimblerig. He joined Davy and Georgie on their trek to Texas. While riding on the plains, they encountered an Indian who was down on his luck and so joined the crew. Suddenly a group of Mexican cavalry appeared and chased our boys until the shots from a fort caused the soldiers to cease their chase.

The fort was the Alamo.

William Travis, in command, told our hero that they were surrounded by a large Mexican army, were vastly outnumbered, and were hoping for reinforcements. The number thrown out by Disney was that there were five thousand Mexicans and less than two hundred Texans. Even as later reading revealed that the Mexican army was about half that, General Santa Anna's army was still much larger than the Alamo's defenders. I thrilled as our boys, shooting with incredible accuracy, stopped the first attack. So far, things looked good. It became clear, however, that there would be no reinforcements and the prospects for the Alamo looked bleak.

To make it clear that their days were numbered, Fess Parker sang a song adapted from a poem actually written by Davy, "Farewell to the Mountains."

Farewell to the mountains, whose mazes to me
Are more beautiful far than Eden could be.
The home I redeemed from the savage and wild.
The home I have loved as a father his child.

(bridge)
The wife of my bosom, Farewell to ye all.
In the land of the stranger, I rise or I fall.

This was getting serious, but surely Davy and company would get out of this jam.

Finally, the attack came and the Alamo was overwhelmed by large numbers of Mexican soldiers. They climbed the walls with siege ladders and rushed in when they battered down the gates. One by one the defenders fell, after they took a Mexican or two with them. First, the Indian, then Thimblerig, who fought more bravely than I expected from his character. Then bullets hit Georgie Russell. His final words: "Give em what fer, Davy." Soon, Davy was the only one left as Mexicans were on all sides of him. The episode ended with Davy swinging his rifle like a baseball bat and the scene blended into the tattered Texas flag and finally, the modern Texas flag.

Yes, it was true. My hero died defending the principles of freedom and the American way. It didn't matter then that the Texans were establishing a nation on Mexican soil, or that the Texans had slavery after slavery was abolished in Mexico. As a boy, all I saw were brave Americans fighting against tremendous odds. I cried when I knew my hero was killed. Regardless of what I later learned, including that Davy was captured then killed after the battle was over, the bravery of those men, fighting in a decaying fort in winter, against odds of at least 10 to 1, and possibly more, still haunts me.

Texas became, to me, the epitome of what is meant to be an American. First, they won their independence from the Mexicans. Then, it was the place captured in so many cowboy movies. As a young boy, I knew nothing about the harassment of the Mexicans in Texas after independence, nor did I think about Texas as a slave state and part of the Confederacy, or a place of Jim Crow laws or right-wing militants. And it was long before JFK was quoted as including Texas as one of the three most overrated things in the world.

"Uncle Fred, I saw this great movie, 'Johnny Tremain,' about a boy who lived in Boston during the Revolutionary War. He carried messages for the Sons of Liberty and fought the Redcoats at Lexington and Concord."

"What did you like about, it? " Fred asked.

"It was about how Americans fought for our freedom from the British. That is how we became a free country. They were very brave. They weren't a real army. They were Minutemen. The British had a strong army and navy but we won the war and got our independence. I like movies about our history."

"Brian, this isn't our history. Our people were in Italy in those days. There were no Italians in the Revolutionary War. Paul Revere and George Washington and those guys weren't Italian."

"No, Uncle Fred," I shouted, "I'm an American. I am not Italian."

"Fred, when I was fighting the Japs during the war, you think I thought that I wasn't fighting for my country because there were no Italians way back then?", my father interjected. He went on about having parents from Italy, yet Italians were the enemy. "When I was processed in boot camp, they asked if I would have a problem fighting Italy. I told the officer, Sir, I am an American and will go where I am sent. I was hoping to be assigned to a gun crew on a merchant ship sailing between New York and England so I could get home once in awhile, but ended up in the Pacific. Let me tell you, Fred," he continued. "When I got a letter from my sister that the church had a dance for the Italian POWs, I got really mad. Here I was fighting against enemy planes and subs and the church I was baptized in had a dance so the Italian girls in the neighborhood could entertain the enemy? I knew then that even though my mother and father were born in Italy and my father was in the Italian military, I was an American and didn't give a shit about Italy." Millie said, "Pete, watch your language." All I thought was that my father and I were Americans. I was proud to be his son.

I had an early interest and love for American history. The first book I read which wasn't a Golden Book or school reader was American history. I borrowed a 90-page book from the "library" in the rear of my first-grade class and read it cover to cover in one night. I still remember the painting of the death of General Wolfe at the battle of Quebec.

I read constantly as a young boy. I gravitated to factual stuff. Our house wasn't loaded with books but there was enough to keep me busy. I had a series of books that contained large stamps that illustrated the subject on each page. "Boats and Ships of the Sea," "American History," and "George Washington" were a few of the titles. The drill was to place the stamp on the appropriate page, then to read the text. We had a set of encyclopedias that I poured through with special attention to American and Roman history.

The word was out that I was a reader. There was not much reading in our circles so there was some innuendo that I was somewhat less than a "real boy." That, of course, offended my parents who never passed on the opportunity to say how I always played with guns, got into a few fights, and loved to play baseball.

In the either/or world of Brooklyn Italian Americans, I was complicated.

Chapter 5. The Extended Family and the Macaroni Kid

Uncle Fred, married to Aunt Rose, the eldest of my mother's siblings, was the respected family authority. Not only was he the oldest, but he actually graduated from high school, a rare feat in the Italian-American community of his era. He had knowledge of worldly things like geography. He was also very opinionated and judgmental. His favorite word was pronounced "gitdrool," the common mispronunciation for the Italian word for cucumber, meaning a dull person with limited intelligence.

"Italy brought civilization to the world. First the Romans conquered the world. They built roads and had running water. Roman buildings are still around today. Then, during the Renaissance, they brought Europe out of the dark ages. They taught us how to eat with a fork. Da Vinci was a genius. Michelangelo painted the ceiling of the Sistine Chapel on his back," opined Uncle Fred.

"I know Italy did great stuff," I replied, "but I am an American."

I did not disagree that many great things came from Italy but these were not my great things. As for contemporary Italians, I was quite uncomfortable when someone was playing Italian language radio. I even hated the Progresso olive oil can. It was covered with a painting of things Italian. It was cluttered and off putting to me. There was a Roman figure on a chariot holding a torch, an airplane, a ship, a sunrise, some buildings--all in garish colors. It was clearly foreign, not modern, not AMERICAN.

Likewise, I had an aversion to actual Italians, thinking that their language was strange and that they were unclean. In the movie "Houseboat," we were supposed to think that Sophia Loren was beautiful. In my young American mind, I was convinced she had bad breath.

Uncle Fred's enthusiasm for things Italian even extended to baseball. In one of our conversations where I told him how much I loved baseball, he replied: "I'm not interested in baseball since Joe D retired." That crossed the line. Baseball was baseball and it was above national origins, race or politics. His comment about Joe DiMaggio was, to me, the equivalent of the girls on the block who grabbed my baseball cards and commented on who was, or wasn't, "cute." Pure ignorance when they favored some utility outfielder with a hundred games under his belt to a star like Duke Snider because of their looks. In all fairness, the Topps 1956 baseball card photos were not the greatest likenesses since my hero, the great Duke of Flatbush, was, in fact, a good looking man, although that didn't mean anything to me at age six.

My mother was the youngest of five siblings. Aunt Rose, her only sister, was the oldest. We spent a great deal of time with Aunt Rose and Uncle Fred and their daughters Louise and Francis. It seemed as if we were at their apartment in Corona, Queens every Sunday after dinner. First church, then macaroni and meatballs, then the cemetery, then the visit. Sundays had a ritualistic feel capped by the feeling of dread about school the next day as the day wore on.

I paid attention to the conversations since there was nothing else to do. The conversations were usually of things that happened in the past. Of more current concern were such issues as to who could look at a woman's body. "Only my husband could see me in a nightgown" was a common quip. One subject for debate was whether it was okay for a doctor to look at a woman. This seemed to be a great concern. They usually settled on such bits of wisdom such as "when a doctor looks at you, he is not a man." That made them feel better, I guess,

That family liked me since I was so polite and so I was included in the conversations. They often played music which, of course, meant

Italian-American singers. That family loved Dean Martin. "Look at his picture," Aunt Rose would say holding up the album cover, "he is sooo handsome." The album of choice was anything that had Italian favorites like "On an Evening in Roma," "Return to Sorrento," or his big hit "That's Amore." The latter is only song I could remember that contained the words "Pasta Fazool." As great as fellow paisan Frank Sinatra was, he didn't sing Italian songs, or American songs with Italian words or references. But when Dino sang, he was one of us:

In the meantime let me tell you that I love you Buona sera signorina kiss me goodnight When Connie Francis and Bobby Darin sang together on some variety show, everyone was excited and hoped that these two young, talented, Italian-Americans would get married. It never happened.

What all my extended family had in common was that they were suckers for any record that had some Italian reference even though they were not actually Italian songs. Since records were available as singles, buying a popular song was not a major expense for people who had to be careful with their money.

"Eh Cumpari" sung by Julius LaRosa was a must have since the lyrics were in Italian and asked about, then mimicked, the sounds of various instruments.

Lou Monte recorded several songs with mixed English and Italian lyrics. Probably the most popular was ""Lazy Mary," sung to the tune of a real Italian song. It was a mix or English and Italian words. What seemed to amuse the grownups was that Mary had to get out of bed because the sheets were needed for the table. While we never ate on sheets someone had just slept in, that did not seem unfamiliar to family members. To me, it sounded like a disgusting thing to do.

While music played a part in our Italian-American culture, the primary focus, the touchstone of right and wrong, and the proof of our superiority, was food. There were so many times at the dinner table when my father would say to me, "When you get married and are out of the house, you think you're gonna eat like this?" Even then, I thought that adult life, freedom from parental control, and having my own place would probably counterbalance the lack of my mother's cooking every night. But to Italians, food had an exalted place, far above mere adulthood and independence.

Food had a meaning behind nutrition. It was how a woman showed she loved her family. The amount of time spent in the kitchen was in direct proportion to a woman's value. I heard many derogatory references to Jewish women who, supposedly, ordered in, or ate out, and therefore, didn't love their children. Aunt Rhoda, however, was said to make good gravy. Even though she was Jewish, she learned from my mother how to cook in order to please Uncle Louie. It was surprising to learn as I got older that food was a major factor in Jewish lives as well and that the term "Jewish mother" did not mean one who didn't care about her kids.

The starting point in our family was the sauce which was called "gravy." The gravy was what covered the macaroni, never referred to as pasta. Every Sunday, the family made the good gravy, the meat sauce. This always consisted of meatballs and sausages. Meatballs themselves required a great deal of work, as well as being the subject of differing recipes. The chopped meat had to be mixed with breadcrumbs, eggs, and seasoning. How much of each to be used was where the subjectivity came into play. Then, they were fried ("browned") before being cooked in the sauce for however long the cook believed was good for both the sauce and for the meat. Usually, the meatballs and the sausages were enhanced by other strange additions under the theory that the more different kinds of meat that was used, the better the gravy. Millie would add a piece of pork, and sometimes braciole, a piece of beef, pounded thin, mixed with a bit of ricotta cheese, pronounced "ragut", and herbs, rolled and cooked in the gravy. Lesser favorites for me were rolled up skin, and neck bones. The skin was just a disgusting roll of fat and only my mother ate it. The neck bones sometimes splintered so I had to be careful of the small pieces in the gravy.

"I like Aunt Lucy's gravy," I told my mother. "Eh, it's OK but she burns the onions." The sad look on her face told me that she was disappointed that I liked another woman's gravy. "Yours is the best, Ma, but I like her gravy too."

I didn't like Aunt Rose's gravy. While my mother ran the stewed tomatoes through a mill so only the sauce would enter the gravy, Aunt Rose put the whole tomato, skin and pulp and seeds, into the mix. As a fussy eater, that was as bad as the splintered neck bones, and I hated to have to pick around certain things on my plate.

Gravy was apparently very sensitive. If not cooked enough it was bitter and tangy. If cooked too much, that was bad too, but I was never sure why. Mother's was just right, of course.

In the days before Vatican II, when meat on Friday's was a sin, she often made marinara sauce, pronounced "madenade." This was only tomato sauce, and was cooked quickly. Marinara was the shorthand for simple, home-cooked fare. When my parents and family members later had the bucks to go to the Pocono's or on a cruise, they would say: "The food was good but I'm in the mood for a little madenade."

Macaroni was not just a matter of taste. It stirred passions. I heard one family member say: "Eww, he put cheese on the madenade. I wanna throw up." Apparently, in that wing of the extended family, grated cheese was only for meat sauce. "Ma, why don't you make ziti instead of spaghetti? It's easier to eat," I asked. "It's delicious," my mother replied. "But the taste is the same, it is only a different shape," I retorted. "It's delicious," she repeated.

No holiday was complete without the macaroni, even those holidays known for other foods. We always had turkey on Thanksgiving, but first the macaroni. Since this was a special occasion, the macaroni had to be special. There was no better first course to an Italian Thanksgiving dinner than some kind of stuffed Italian dish.

Lasagna was a common favorite. So before the turkey, stuffing, potatoes and vegetables, we had a nice square of lasagna along with the "gravy meat" in case there was a possibility of leaving the table without having enough to eat.

Any meal that involved guests included the macaroni and gravy meat course. People who weren't used to eating this way had their fill of the first course that was always well prepared and tasty. What they didn't know after some stuffed shells or manicotti ("manigut") and a few meatballs, was that a roast of some sort was next, along with potatoes and vegetables. For good measure, the vegetables were often breaded and fried. I recall the look of shock and often embarrassment on the part of the guests who knew they could not possibly do justice to the well-prepared and labor-intensive bounty in front of them.

Mother, of course, enjoyed the praise of the non-Italian guests who had never eaten like that before, but also that of family members who had, therefore affirming her status as the best cook in the family.

As an American kid, I thought the turkey and side dishes were plenty but to our family, the macaroni was essential. It was not a mortal sin not to serve it but perhaps a venial sin which would land you in purgatory, but not hell.

No one in the family ever bought a bottle of wine. If there was wine in the house, it was home made by a relative or by some other connection. The wine was dark red and so dense that no light could pass through. Uncle Fred would drink it in full water tumblers explaining "This is food." My mother would mix it with cream soda. Many houses and apartments smelled of that wine. There was a wine press in our cellar but it was not used any more. Mother would talk about how the men, including her father, would buy a shipment of grapes and press it in the cellar and test it now and then until it was ready for a wider distribution.

In our family, at least, the kids weren't given wine. We were, however, given all the macaroni and meatballs we wanted. In my case, it was a moderate amount. Cousin Vito ate more than I did and, therefore, earned the valued title of the "Macaroni Kid." On one special occasion, he ate six ravioli to my two, resulting in shame that I carried all my life.

No one bought ravioli in a store. It had to be home made. Since it was so labor intensive, it required the work of several women. First, the dough was made and kneaded until it could be stretched over a large board. The ricotta was placed a few inches apart and the dough folded over. Then, a water glass was used to mold the cheese into a circle and to size the ravioli. The size was large. Finally, the creations were place in large pots of boiling water and cooked. Considering the size of these things, two of them, and an accompanying meatball, was a substantial dinner for a small boy but I was still ashamed that Vito ate six. He wasn't a fat kid but just had more of an appetite. I always thought the family liked him more because of his eating but I learned much later that he didn't agree with my youthful analysis.

As a young boy, I was not adventurous about food. I was good with Italian staples like macaroni with meatballs and gravy, and with American food like steak, hamburgers, hot dogs and peanut butter and jelly sandwiches. While we never went to restaurants that served anything exotic, I had an experience one Christmas Eve that taught me that there was more to food than what I was getting from my family, both immediate, or closely extended.

We were invited to the home of my mother's cousin. To that point, Christmas Eve was either at my house, or one other familiar relative. I did not know Jerry or his wife Connie. My mother said that Connie was Sicilian, not that it meant anything to me what part of Italy anyone came from. Italian was Italian, or so I thought.

Apparently, Sicilians had their own set of customs for Christmas Eve. Connie took literally that Christmas Eve was the Feast of the Seven Fishes. I never saw so much fish in my life or so many dishes that I found repulsive. While I could eat my mother's breaded and fried flounder with no problems, Connie's feast consisted of stuffed claims, dried codfish ("bacala"), shrimp, scallops, squid, and other kinds of shellfish. I was urged by Connie to try this, try that, but to my seven year old palate, it was all a disgusting mess. Looking back, I realized all the preparation that went into that feast and how I would love to be seated at that table now, but as an American kid, I saw that some people were even more Italian than my family. I was actually comforted by the knowledge that we were less Italian and, therefore more American, than others.

Since my mother and father had many siblings, I had many aunts, uncles and cousins. Three of my mother's siblings lived within walking distance so I saw my uncles, aunts and cousins almost every day. Uncle Louie's chrome dinette store on the ground floor of our house was a focal point of our little village which added to the sense of proximity. In addition to my blood relatives, their spouses all had families nearby so there was an additional layer of consanguinity, which meant another bunch of people to judge, to be judged by, and to gossip about. Of course, these were more people around whom I had to behave in a way that would not shame my mother.

Uncle Mike's wife, Aunt Francesca, was born in Italy. English was, therefore, her second language, which she spoke with a heavy accent. Their two children, Theresa and another Vito, spoke Italian before they spoke English. When I referred to them as "my Italian cousins," my mother always snapped "They were born HERE."

They may have been born in the good old USA but their behavior and attitudes were very much of the old country due to the time they spent with their mother's family, all Italian speakers, with the requisite old world baggage concerning evil eyes and other superstitions. Vito was about two years younger than me but he seemed like he was from another planet. He didn't play ball with my other cousin Vito and me, and would hang around the older people joining their conversations, if not in Italian, then in English punctuated with Italian expressions.

"Porca la miseria," he would frequently say which, as explained by Uncle Fred, meant as a general complaint about how bad the world is. Years later, when he was around 11 and I had escaped to the suburbs, the cousins were sitting around playing music. Obviously not a fan of our taste, he announced to all those present, "Eh, how come ya lissnin to rock and roll? Play Jimmy Roselli."

Vito and Theresa did not act like American kids. They would not eat a hamburger or hot dog. They only ate what their mother cooked. And Aunt Francesca only cooked pasta that she made herself, from scratch. Years later, at a catered engagement party for an older cousin, we were sitting at the kids' table and were served prime rib. Vito exclaimed "You call dis food? I trow up over dis food." When I told him to quiet down, his sister intervened, but not to chastise her brother for loutish behavior. Her response to me was, "You don't tell us what to do. Only our mother tells us what to do. I'll throw this roast beef in your face."

They had emotional breakdowns when they were separated from their mother so their parents could not leave them with anyone. For the other Vito and me, as well as Jessica, it was a treat to sleep at a cousin's house when our parents had a rare night out. Not for Vito and Theresa. They were rewarded for their rigid inability to adjust to the slightest change in their daily routine by their parents taking them to family weddings to which the kids were not invited. "It's not fair that they get to go to weddings and we don't." I complained. "They can't stay anywhere but their own house or they cry and throw up," Mother replied. My sense of justice was offended. Here I was, the good boy who almost never made a scene, and those two got to go to weddings! Having never been to one, I imagined all the fun and glamour of everyone dressed up in their finest Brooklyn clothes, dancing to a band. I always had a sense that there was a whole world I was missing, like what was on TV when I was asleep.

Theresa was superstitious due to the amount of time she spent with her mother's aunt who knew the entire litany of Italian curses and taboos. It was bad luck to look a man with crutches, or in a cast. When Uncle Fred broke his leg when hit by a car on his postal route, she could not be in the same room with him. Not that she would provide much company or comfort in any event. The poor man was hospitalized for weeks and on sick leave for months. We visited often, as did other family members, but Theresa lived in her own world. It was politically correct for the aunts to make the best of her behavior or, for that matter, the bad or strange behavior of any kid, by stating, with no evidence whatsoever: "She's gonna grow up to be a beautiful young lady." As it happened, that wasn't the case.

The reader might be curious as to what became of Theresa in the years after we left the old neighborhood.

After Catholic elementary school when her father sat with her and her brother to do homework, she dropped out of high school, then attended a beauty academy and left there because she fought with everyone. She got pregnant, married Frankie, and had a boy. Eager to have a girl she could raise in her own image, she continued to have babies and ended up with four boys. Realizing that this was a losing battle, in the church for a wedding of another cousin, she announced to my father, "Uncle Pete, I got my tubes tied."

"Aunt Millie, how long do you fry the meatballs before you put them in the gravy," asked my cousin Loretta. Since she lived across the street and her father's store was downstairs, she was often in our apartment talking to my mother about various things. Mother was the only high school graduate among her siblings and was considered the smart and classy one, a lady, as many said. She was the person to come to with questions about cooking, clothes, dating, and in Loretta's case, about her mother and father. "My father is always screaming about something. Last night, I had a date to go to a movie. Billy came up to the apartment and he started yelling. "You're going out with a guy with pimples? You can't go out with my daughter. Get outta here." "Aunt Millie, I ran to my room and cried all night. My mother is so afraid of him. She didn't say nothing. She is a very stupid woman. I feel like I have nobody to turn to." "I'll talk to him" is all Mother had to say.

Later that night, Mother told my father about the conversation. He too was very fond of Loretta. "Louie is a nut. I'd like to punch him in the mouth the way he treats those girls." "Whaddya gonna do?" Mother replied, "He's my brother."

Our place was an island of sanity for Loretta. She came every Christmas morning. She helped out at all the birthday parties. When my father bought a movie camera, she was there for the first reel. I, the ever obedient son, took very seriously the instructions that this was a movie camera so I had to move. "Are you going to dance? Are you going to jump?" asked Mother. I decided I would jump. So, in the whole reel, I jumped up and down looking like a kid with ADD or as they put it then, with ants in my pants. But there was Loretta, pushing Jessica on a swing set my parents bought, holding her for a close up, and in general, acting like we were the family she would rather be with.

Loretta and Marie were teenagers and I was five when Aunt Rhoda got pregnant. Being Italian, Uncle Louie was praying for a son. When the baby was born, it was, indeed, the son he was waiting for after 13 years. He spray painted the garage doors leading to his shop on the first floor of our house "Its a boy." "King Louis, 6 pounds 7 ounces." The artwork was topped with, a crown. Since our family owned the building, the graffiti was not considered vandalism. Besides, no sign of celebration was out of line when welcoming a boy to an Italian-American family.

We all fussed over little Louie. Since most of the family, on both the father's and mother's side, were in walking distance, the newest addition got a lot of attention. With two teenage sisters, he did not lack for hands on care, nor did it ever happen that he didn't get his way. Vito and I played with him but were too young to care for him but the females in his life catered to anything and everything. "Loretta, go home and get my skates," he said when a few years older. "I'm not getting your skates," the usually indulgent sister replied. "If you don't get my skates, I'm gonna throw myself on the floor," King Louie retorted. It was then that my mother explained to me what a spoiled child was.

While my father's family did not move off the geographic location of Long Island, they were no longer within walking distance of each other, so they took great efforts to get together regularly. Even though Brooklyn and Queens were on Long Island, we only considered Long Island to be the non New York City counties of Nassau and Suffolk, aka "the Island."

The grownups had regular evening gatherings taking turns every few months at one of the houses of the brothers and sisters. For the kids, there were at least two family picnics every summer. At first, we went to Hempstead Lake State Park. As the brothers began to migrate to "the Island" the picnics moved to Salsbury Park, which was more exclusive since it was limited to residents of Nassau County. The residents were allowed one guest car, so we followed one of my uncles who emigrated from Brooklyn before we did.

I really looked forward to those picnics, especially to play with my cousin Michael. We didn't have a budget for vacations so day trips to the beach or family picnics were the extent of summer outings. The brothers and brothers in law were young enough to engage in spirited softball games while the women, of course, tended to the cooking. Since these were always on Sunday, macaroni had to be part of the meal. It took a long time to boil water on outdoor fires but no one saw any reason why this Sunday should be different from any other Sunday. The woman also brought foods that they cooked at home and only needed to heat in the park. So, in addition to the macaroni, there were sausages, eggplant parmagiana, and various other Italian foods to share. The evening meal was the more traditional hamburgers and hot dogs.

Uncle Eddie, married to my father's sister Nettie, was a big man with a huge belly and a prodigious appetite. He came with a Coca Cola cooler made out of heavy metal, filled with beer. Michael and I tried to count how many 48 ounce bottles of Rheingold he consumed but lost count if we turned away or engaged in other activities. Despite the beer, he ate quantities that everyone talked about. Overeating was not a shameful thing in those days so for people to notice, he had to consume the intake of say, a family of four, assuming none of the four were picky eaters. I guess carrying that cooler and his job in the soap factory made him incredibly strong. Despite his girth, he played softball with the guys and hit some tremendous drives.

As the day turned to dusk, the adults would hang around the picnic tables singing and otherwise embarrassing the kids. Eddie would stand on the table and sing "I wanna dance with the dolly with a hole in her stockin, heel keeps a knockin, toes keep a rockin, I wanna dance with the dolly with the hole in her stockin, dance by the light of the moon." This became a ritual so at every picnic, someone said, "Hey, Eddie, sing 'Dolly with a hole in her stockin." It wasn't until I was an adult that a learned that the title of the song that contained that lyric was "Buffalo Gal." This was hardly the only bit of misinformation I heard as a kid. The older boys on the block once talked about a song called "The Aler Rose of Texas." Of course, song titles were the least of what I heard that was wrong, either factually, or because the truth had to be hidden, like where babies came from.

Since family picnics were definitely considered a successful effort with my father's family, Mother attempted to organize them with her family. This group, however, was not as good with cooperative efforts. It was not possible to get a softball game going, or even to have everyone show up on time for the caravan from Brooklyn to Hempstead Lake State Park. Aunt Fran's tripe didn't go over too well with the kids.

I didn't think sandy rubber band was a taste to strive for but the adults, at least some of them, found this non traditional picnic fair something to get excited about.

The final insult, literally, from above, was that every one of these few attempts ended in a rain storm, although one, before I was born, was etched in the family memory as the greatest day ever. It was held in Astoria Park and was sheltered from the rain by the Triborough Bridge. There were no deaths in the immediate family then and Millie, her sister and brothers would talk about it as one of the great times in their lives. "Remember the picnic under the bridge," Mother would say. "We had so much fun. Papa played the mandolin and we all sang. It didn't matter that it rained." Her voice chocked up and her eyes began to water as she recalled a happy time that could never be reproduced because of the missing persons.

As the better organized and more cooperative side, my father's family also had occasional banquet dinners for the grown ups and the kids. These took place at the restaurant in what was originally Salsbury Park, later changed to Eisenhower Park. We had a room of our own and there were usually about 30 of us in attendance. In those days, of course, these were jacket and tie functions. As a stuffy kid, I was drawn to the dignity of my father's family. There was never any shouting or loud talk. Table manners were good. In short, we acted like Americans.

Millie tried once to replicate these events with her family. The results were, as expected, quite different. The selection was an Italian restaurant in a townhouse in Brooklyn. I remember that it looked classy, with white table cloths and a subdued decor. The waiters wore tuxedos and the pumped in music was classical piano, no Dean Martin. At least I thought it was classical but it may have been piano versions of standards. This was not the kind of place my family was used to.

As usual, Uncle Louie showed up late so dinner was delayed. When he got there, he talked so loud that he could be heard all over the restaurant, even in the adjoining room. "Louie, everybody in restaurant can hear you," Mother said. His response: "Wha, I gotta sit here like a mamaluke?"

Instead of a banquet, everyone ordered individually so it took forever to eat. Uncle Fred gave a long list of demands. "First, I want spaghetti. I want the meatballs and sausages on the side. Bring a glass of wine now." My father, sensitive to the impending chaos said that Fred thought he was eating Sunday dinner at home. ""Fred is not used to eating at restaurants. He's too cheap to go out," Father said. Mother witnessed the turmoil and saw the adults were served while the kids were waiting for their food. She would not admit that her family was not the kind you could take out. "Louie was talking so loud, he was embarrassing. Fran doesn't eat anything that she doesn't cook herself. Her kids think anything she doesn't make is poison. Fred complained about everything. Thank God, my kids know how to act." Father replied, "That's because we do everything right so our kids know how to act in a restaurant."

I thought that I knew how to act in a restaurant because I was not Italian. I was an American kid.

Chapter 6. The Regular Guy

In our neighborhood, we didn't allow eccentricities. No one was artistic, intellectual, politically rebellious, sensitive, or different in any way. At least, that was the face put on for the public. The worst thing was to be called a sissy mary. Later, of course, I thought back and realized that the boy, who was obsessed with female movie stars, and not in a lustful way, was gay. At eight years old, I didn't know who Rhonda Fleming was, but Jerry did. But in our world, it was important to be a real boy, one who would grow up into a regular guy.

Jerry was mild kid. Even though, on our block, there were occasional challenges to one's toughness, resulting in an occasional fist fight, Jerry seemed immune from such challenges. He was nice to everyone. Unlike most of the boys, he never made a nasty remark or wisecrack. He didn't join any game that required a ball, but would play hide and seek and other street games. I hung with him in his apartment on occasion. We looked at his movie star cards, played board games and listened to his mother's records, which included Red Foxx's raunchy comedy album. Jerry did not fit the mold of a real boy as defined in the neighborhood but because he was nice, and kind, he was not called on to stand up to the other boys.

The neighborhood was filled with regular guys, those who started out as real boys. My father was one. Few, if any, graduated from high school, and many didn't even attend. They were mostly World War II veterans. My father served on a destroyer escort in the South Pacific. He was intelligent enough to qualify for the highly technical job as a radar/sonar operator, the eyes and ears warning the ship of attacking planes, ships, and submarines. I heard the stories of his ship sinking a Japanese submarine, shooting down enemy planes, or picking up downed pilots out of the ocean. At Okinawa, the Japs used kamikazes to crash into American ships, taking a large toll of men and ships. He spotted one coming at his ship in time for the gunners to shoot it down. It crashed close enough to create a wave that rocked the ship. He and his shipmates survived that terrible battle. He returned safely to Brooklyn, to his mother, and to his girlfriend Millie. In later years, when he talked about Okinawa, his eyes watered at the memory of his twenty-year-old self facing death in one of history's greatest naval battles.

These regular guys read *The Daily News*, a tabloid written for the working people of the City. That paper had a roving photographer feature where people on the street were interviewed about the issues of the day. Uncle Mike was featured one day and asked what the U.S. should do about Cuba, shortly after Castro came to power. "Bomb 'em." was his solution. "That goes for Russia too. We take too much guff from them." That kind of sentiment permeated that newspaper in that era, where letters to the editor were often signed "Fed up" and "Disgusted." Any hint of peaceful coexistence was met by accusations of being a "Commie" or, at least, a "Pinko."

The main interest of *The Daily News*, however, was the Brooklyn Dodgers.

In those days, New York City had three baseball teams, the Dodgers, the New York Giants, and the New York Yankees. There were great rivalries. The Dodgers and the Giants in the regular season and the Dodgers and the Yankees in the World Series. Each team had its successes, but none more successful than the Yankees, which won the World Series five years in a row, three times over the Dodgers in that stretch and once over the Giants. The rivalries were boisterous and personal. Despite the myths of later years, not everyone in Brooklyn was a Dodgers fan. Two of my uncles were Giants fans and there were a number Yankees fans lording it over the Dodgers fans about our team never winning a World Series. At the start of a World Series between the Dodgers and the Yankees, some of the older kids on the block hung an effigy of the Dodgers manager, Walter Alston, "Wait Till Next Year" was the cry of futility until, finally, in 1955, the Brooklyn Dodgers were world champs. There were parties in the streets. Fans of other teams congratulated Dodger fans as if it was their personal achievement. Perhaps it was. During my father's lifetime, the Dodgers lost to the Yankees in the World Series five times before the Holy Year of 1955. His pain and suffering was finally over. When he told me that Duke Snider hit four homeruns, the Duke became my favorite ballplayer for the rest of my life.

During the following season, I followed every game in the newspaper by reading *The Daily News* from the back, where the sports section started. I knew every player's batting average, cheered Duke Snider as he led the league in homeruns, heard Jackie Robinson's last homerun on the radio, and saw his last hit on TV, a game winning drive in the World Series that the Dodgers lost, once again, to the Yankees.

The Dodgers brought people together regardless of ethnicity or religion. African Americans rooted for Jackie Robinson. The Catholic newspaper wrote glowingly about Gil Hodges, an Irish Catholic, but for real fans, it didn't matter. They were our team. They made us proud.

My father not only lived and breathed baseball, he also played. He was the speedy second baseman of his high school team who specialized in bunting, hit and run, and those things that made baseball the game that God created. He taught me the game. It was important, he said, to be able to hit and throw. "If guys play ball at a picnic, you don't wanna throw like this," making a sissy-like motion that we called throwing like a girl.

Two years after winning the World Series, it became apparent that the Dodgers were going to move to Los Angeles. This was an act of treason worthy of Benedict Arnold. The Dodgers owner, Walter O'Malley, was reviled in Brooklyn for generations. When asked who the worst persons in history were, Brooklynites still answer: "Hitler, Stalin, and Walter O'Malley."

Being a good American father, with a good American son, Peter took me to see my first major league game at Ebbets Field in their final season of 1957. I was awed at all the green grass and the famous scoreboard and chain link fence in right field. The Dodgers beat the Cincinnati Redlegs 8-0 but I was disappointed that Duke didn't get a hit.

The Dodgers had a young left fielder named Gino Cimoli. He had a good year that season. He was considered handsome and because he was Italian, everybody talked about him. "Cimoli is a good looking guy," according to Uncle Louie. Cousin Loretta went further, "I don't care about baseball but Gino Cimoli is so cute." She doesn't care about baseball? That is a heresy that was barely excusable in a girl but not so in a boy. I tried to explain that he was a good player but Snider, Hodges, and Furillo were all much better. What kind of world was this where a person didn't care about baseball but judged a player by his looks? I attributed only that girls didn't know anything about what was really important. I blamed this on her being Italian and believed that real American girls, like the ones I saw on TV, understood baseball.

Like a good American boy, I was obsessed with baseball statistics. They were obtained mostly from the back of baseball cards since there was no internet with all the numbers I would ever have needed. I knew all of Duke Snider's stats by heart. I knew the batting crown winners year by year. I could name all the players with more than 300 homers, a much smaller number of players in those days. Who cared about their color or their ethnic background? Everyone argued about which of the centerfielders of the New York teams, Duke Snider of the Dodgers, Willie Mays of the Giants, or Mickey Mantle of the Yankees, was the best. When they all played in New York, a case could be made for each of them. "Mays hit 51 homers last year," one uncle would say. "He is a showoff, always losing his hat," my father would reply. "And Snider led the league in RBIs. That's what wins ballgames."

Baseball was very personal in Brooklyn. When the Giants won the 1954 World Series, my father shook hands and congratulated his brother, the Giants fan, as if he was the winner.

My father told me stories about his heroes in the earlier years. "My favorite player was Dolph Camilli. He was Italian but that didn't really matter to us. He was their best home run hitter," he would say. "Baseball was our life back then."

"There was a Jewish girl in my class who always talked about workers and Communism. We would tease her. She said 'All you American boys think about is baseball.' We said that if everyone thought about baseball, we would be better off." My father admitted that they were just kids then. Besides who would have a serious conversation with a girl about politics?

As kids, we didn't actually see much baseball. We couldn't watch day games on TV because we were at school. We couldn't watch more than an inning or two at night because we had to go to bed. Each morning, I would run down to my uncle's store below our apartment and ask him how the Dodgers did and if Duke Snider hit any homeruns. I would then read his *Daily News* from the back to study the box score and the standings. Mostly, however, I learned baseball through baseball cards. They came in backs of five or six for a nickel, and included a flat piece of pink bubblegum. I started collecting the 1956 series which had a picture of the player's face with some action shot in the background. The reverse side had some information about the player including his statistics for the previous year and his lifetime totals. It was really exciting when I opened a pack and found stars like Ted Williams, Mickey Mantle, Willie Mays, or my favorite, Duke Snider. Of course, there was a card for each player so we were as likely to get a card for a part time utility infielder as we would for a star.

Since there was no guarantee that we would get new cards in each pack, we set aside "doubles" for flipping. This was a game where we dropped a card in a way that made it tumble. If you matched the heads or tails of the cards your opponent threw down, you won those cards. With practice, I could hold a card a certain way, heads or tails, and flip it exactly the same way each time and would get the desired head or tail. As we advanced, we played two or three cards at a time. If a player was really good, they would make all heads or all tails. The odds against three of the same from the opponent were fairly high so it was a sign of a good player to be able to present all cards of one side.

The 1957 series of cards was better produced. Instead of the standard head shot that had been used several years in a row, these cards had a full picture of the player in an action pose, at bat, or in the field. The back side had the player's entire year by year statistics. Of course, I poured over them incessantly so, throughout my life, I could remember how many home runs Ted Kluszewski hit in 1953, 54, 55, and 56. This stuff never impressed anyone's mother. The rote response was "if you spent as much time on your homework as on those stupid cards..." Mothers, however, got their revenge as I would learn later that everyone's mother threw out those cards at some point in later years when we weren't looking.

As regular guys, we didn't just talk about games, we played them. Our games had to be adapted to the Brooklyn streets. The only place where we could play hardball was in the large schoolyard of the nearby junior high school. "The kids on Long Island are all good 'cause they got alotta places to play," I said. I am not sure what made me think that but I knew there was a golden land, not far away, where real Americans lived. There were fields to play ball and everyone lived in a house with no one upstairs or downstairs. And everyone was white.

We played punch ball. It had the same basic rules as baseball except that we punched a ball with our fists and ran the bases. "We gotta use a spaldeen," cousin Vito insisted, "cause it goes far when you punch it."

A "spaldeen" was a pink rubber ball with "Spalding" written on it, that was a legendary high bouncer when it was new. Vito and I were a team and we never lost a game even against some of the guys that had a reputation of being good players. Since our field was the wide sidewalk on Atlantic Avenue in front of my house, the many balls that landed in the street were hit by cars and sometimes traveled blocks away. We never had a spare ball and, besides, a spaldeen was too valuable to let go, so the game would be delayed until we tracked down the ball. Vito was able to punch the ball farther than me so our strategy was for me to punch a single and for him to blast one over everyone's head for a home run.

We played stick ball too. There were two variations. One was played just like punch ball except the ball was pitched on one bounce and we swung with a stick and ran the bases. A real good player was known as a "two sewer guy." That meant he could hit a ball past two manhole covers. None of my group of young boys could do that but some of the "big guys," those in their early teens could reach that pinnacle of status on Fermi Place. The other variation was played against a wall with a strike zone drawn in chalk. Singles, doubles, triples, and home runs were measured by predetermined locations. "If the ball goes across the street over the garage doors, it's a homer," was the kind of rule we played under. Making good contact with a broom handle and a spaldeen that could take weird bounces wasn't easy. Even when the ball was actually hit, it was more likely to spin and bounce back than reach a hit destination,

A game that required less real estate was stoop ball. We threw a ball against one of the many stoops on our block. If you caught it on one bounce, it was five points, on the fly it was ten, and if it hit the edge it would come back faster and be worth a hundred points. If we missed, the opponent got his turn.

The girls had their games too but as regular guys, we didn't participate in jump rope or any game where they bounced a ball reciting their name, their husband's name, where they came from, and what they sold, in alphabetical order. "A my name is Anna, and my husband's name is Al, and we come from Alabama and we sell apples." It was sissy to play with girls so we teased them and debated who was more stupid.

We didn't play with girls, but somehow, Adeline, the girl next door, was considered to be my girlfriend. Since this was pre puberty, it did not mean much to have a girlfriend. For some unknown reason, I decided to end this relationship. Her friend Vita said, "Brian, Adeline is so upset that she is shaking." Without the empathy I learned later in life, I didn't renege, enjoying the knowledge that I had such power over someone. Adeline was a nice girl, fully Italian, and quite pretty so there was no good reason to break up our innocent relationship. Perhaps it was due to my membership, even leadership, in the He Man Women Haters Club, influenced by the Our Gang Comedies then being shown on TV. That was probably the last time I let Spanky and Alfalfa influence my life.

I did have crushes on girls. There was Alvera, a sixth grader four or five years ahead of me in school. She was very popular with the boys in my class. I was in heaven when she walked with my mother and me to our released time religious instructions on a Wednesday afternoon. My mother said to her in a baby voice: "Are you the girl that all the little boys like?" While Alvera just smiled I was humiliated that my mother would talk to this mature woman in a baby voice. What was she thinking?

There was also Patience and Prudence, two young sisters who at ages 11 and 14 had a hit song "Tonight You Belong to Me." When I said I hated them, I really meant that I liked them and was jealous that they were stars and I was not. I could not admit that I actually liked these two girls.

Then there was Annette Funicello from "The Mickey Mouse Club" who also appeared in the "Spin and Marty" serial that ran on that show.

As was the case with Patience and Prudence, I was jealous that kids around my age were on TV and were famous while I was stuck in Brooklyn, not on TV, not famous, and clearly underappreciated. I even had a dream that Vito and I were in the serial and were greeted by Annette. I woke up too soon from that dream.

Another huge influence was The Three Stooges. One of the local channels, hosted by "Officer" Joe Bolton, showed old shorts in the afternoon. Moe, Larry, and Curley became our touchstones for humor. Vito and I imitated Curley constantly, driving our mothers crazy. Mothers and girls thought they were stupid. They just didn't get humor. I still think that among the differences between men and women is that women don't get The Three Stooges and call all warships "battleships."

The guys played war games but since no one wanted to be the Germans or the Japs, we fought against imaginary enemies. I was a stickler for historical accuracy. When cousin Vito and I played World War II, I made sure that there was a point when we specifically transitioned from the WWI helmets used at the beginning of the war to the newer models. "Look, we have new helmets," I said, in order to make sure our imaginary battles were historically accurate. When we played WWI, we ran in short quick steps the way it appeared in the old newsreels, not knowing that this was the result of slow film, not a special way of movement in that war.

What really pissed me off was when we played at wars from the single shot era. Some of the guys would borrow my Disney licensed Davy Crockett rifle and repeatedly pull the hammer back, fire, and repeat. They didn't understand that after each shot, the ball and powder had to be reloaded and rammed down the barrel before you could fire again. After all, what was the point of war games if we didn't do it right?

My sense of perfection was also in play with miniature soldiers. I had all varieties, modern, the old West, and medieval. The modern ones came with vehicles such as tanks, armored cars, and Jeeps. The ones from the West were part of a set that included a fort of interlocking metal walls, painted like the stockades portrayed in movies. Some soldiers were on horseback, some on foot, and the same for the Native Americans which were called Indians then and were always the enemy.

"Vito, wanna play with my men?" "Yeah, could you set up your fort?" he answered. So I did. It took about a minute to fit the walls together and we were ready for action. He then did the outrageous. He actually placed the medieval figures along with their weapons and horses, outside the clearly apparent nineteenth century western fort. "Vito, we can't use these guys with the calvary fort." To me mixing eras was even worse than mixing troops of different scales. Why couldn't everyone see things, my way, the right way?

There were no rules about realistic looking toy guns so most of us had an arsenal of weapons. The officially licensed Davy Crockett rifle was obviously a toy. Some of my other weapons looked real and could get me shot today if I were a young African-American male. I had a silver six shooter, a 45 army style pistol, and a World War II vintage carbine. My favorite, however, was a Thompson submachine gun, the "tommy gun" made famous in gangster movies. By pulling back the bolt and squeezing the trigger, the gun fired an impressive burst of noise. Cousin Michael had a 50 caliber machine gun mounted on a tripod that shot plastic bullets that glowed in the dark. Parents weren't afraid that we would become war mongers. This is what real American boys did, and besides, who knew when we would be called upon to fight Communists, whether of the Russian or Chinese variety?

"Dad, could we win a war against Russia?" "We have Russia surrounded," was his comforting reply. With the Cold War in full swing, we heard much about Russia's bombers and tanks and about Hungarian refugees after the USSR crushed the revolt in Budapest. My concern, however, was our weaponry. My father told me that his destroyer escort had 20 millimeter guns and 40 millimeter guns and three-inch guns. I didn't know how much a millimeter was but asked how a gun can only be three inches. He explained that this measured the opening of the bore and that the Navy had five-inch guns too and that battleships had sixteen-inch guns! Knowing that American ships had guns that size made me feel much safer. Ever the strategist, I suggested to Vito that we should build fifty atomic battleships. One named after every state. At the time I didn't understand that the government actually had to pay to have things built or that no battleships were built after World War II.

"Uncle Frank wants to take us to the Navy Yard on Saturday," my father said one day. Frank was a welder and worked on the ships, usually aircraft carriers, being built in Brooklyn during the height of the Cold War. The place was enormous. Aside from the ships under construction, there were older WWII ships being repaired or modified. Docked that day, was a cruiser, some support ships, an old submarine, and the newly built aircraft carrier, the Saratoga. My uncle said we could go on the Saratoga today. Cousin Vito and I were about as excited as we could possibly have been to board this huge vessel. There was all sorts of talk about how many football fields could be contained on the flight deck and how many planes the ship could carry. "We have all these carriers," my father said. "Russia doesn't have any." The superiority of our navy compared to the USSR was very comforting. I knew they would be in for it if they messed with our navy. We had the latest and best ships and more of them. So why were we worried about Russia?

The drive home was filled with superlatives, the biggest, the bests, the mosts. We were proud American boys and couldn't wait to get home to play with our models of some of those same ships. My favorite was of the battleship USS Missouri, painted and mounted on a wood base by an older cousin. Of course, we had visions of serving on those ships some day, just as our fathers did not very long before.

Brooklyn was not only home to a great naval ship facility; there was also an air base, Floyd Bennett Field. Our navy not only had ships, it had aircraft and, so, it had air shows. We drove the few miles from our house to see the spectacle of jets, patrol planes, and helicopters flying overhead and to board some of the aircraft on the ground. As a proud American boy, I was impressed by this display of our military might. My father saw this as something a boy should see but he was never a rabid advocate of military things. He served in the US Navy in World War II and saw heavy combat as a 20 year old at the invasions of Japanese held islands. "When Truman dropped the bomb, I believe that saved my life," he told me. "We were getting ready to invade Japan. The way the Japanese fought on all those islands, imagine how they would fight in their homeland?" "We could beat them if we invaded, right?" I asked. "I guess so but we would have lost thousands of guys. They never surrendered so we woudda had to blast them out house by house. And they were giving weapons to women so we would have to shoot women too. Thank God, the war ended before that happened."

My father and I did many guy things apart from military shows. Since we lived in a tough neighborhood, he thought it was important to be able to defend yourself so you don't get pushed around on the street. He said that if I ever came home crying from a fight, he would give me something else to cry about. So he gave me boxing lessons. I learned about leading with my left and hitting hard with my right, about how hitting the nose can really hurt a kid, and that I should keep punching and never try to hold someone's arms. He seemed proud when at age 7 or so; I hit him with a hard right and bloodied his nose.

As a kid, I got into fights for reasons I didn't know. It seemed that kids tested other kids. Sometimes a kid would say "Tommy wants to fight you," and there was no way around the altercation. Once, some girl told one of the kids "Brian wants to fight you," which wasn't the case. Fortunately, I held my own so I wasn't bullied. More fortunately, we moved before I was old enough to get into fights that could cause damage.

My father and I did many father son things. His father, of course, never played with his sons so I guess Dad was his own role model, a real break from his Italian upbringing. We often played catch since he thought it was important to be able to play baseball. Not to be a professional, but to be a regular guy when other regular guys want to play.

From our vantage point on the garage roof on a major thoroughfare, we watched hundreds of cars go by. It became a game to identify the make and the year. In the 1950s, all cars did not look alike. And each year, the cars had a distinctive look. I could identify Ford products from the round tail lights and Chrysler products from the fins. The others were General Motors models. There was a very rare "foreign" car, either an occasional VW "beetle" or an English Hillman. The foreign cars were small and we considered them a joke. The best cars were American and we were proud of what our great country produced.

Despite my admiration for my father and how much I enjoyed our time together, I did not want his life. On a sunny Saturday, he would fix things around our building, touch up paint somewhere, or do something with the car. This was a boring ordinary life, a life I could not imagine living. At that point in my life, I had no role model or contact regarding what else to do on Saturday. In the summer, we may have gone to the beach and there were occasional excursions to Manhattan ("New York") usually around Christmas to see the tree at Rockefeller Center, or rides to various places on Long Island but I saw daily life as too humdrum for someone like me, a real American with hope for the future. I wanted to be a regular guy, but there were limits.

One of the limits was the CYO day camp. Our mothers signed up Vito and me for two weeks at the Catholic Youth Organization camp in Whitestone, Queens. The brochures promised all sorts of activities so it looked promising. When I arrived by the camp bus, I found myself among hundreds of boys at picnic tables. We started with prayers, then paper cups of "bug juice" thus learning my first camp term. I realized that I hated large group activities. I hated to be one of a mass of kids. I found my fellow campers to be rather dull and ordinary. Hold your tongue, one said to me, and say "My father works in a ship yard. He picks up ashes." Wow, I thought, how creative to try to get me to say "shit" and "asses." Even at eight years old, I had an ear for banality. It rained on several of the days so we had a rainy day program which consisted of being herded into a public school where there were options of games in the gym or watching movies in the auditorium. I usually opted for the movies so I didn't have to deal with my fellow campers, who I found totally uninteresting.

Since the boys at CYO came from sections of Brooklyn and Queens other than my neighborhood, they were mostly white and, of course, Catholic. They were more homogenous than my schoolmates. Yet, I found them to be disappointing, adding to my existential dilemma as to my place in my country and the world.

"Always be yourself. You never know who you'll run into," my father told me one day. Of course I am myself, who else will I be, I thought? It seemed that in the neighborhood, it was common for people who were generally of low status, to make up stories about themselves or their possessions. When Uncle Mike inherited some money from his father in law and moved to the tree-lined environs of Richmond Hill, he also bought new furniture, usually ornate pieces with gold painted trim that were a postman's idea of elegant. He would point to a table, or a vase, or some other decor item and declare "You can't buy this in this country." "Dad, if he can't buy those things in this country, where did he buy them?" My mother intervened to say that Uncle Mike likes to exaggerate to make himself feel important.

There were other men who would talk about how they were in charge of people at their factory, or how people admired their cars. In fact, when someone bought a new car, it was customary to tie a red bow to the steering wheel and stand in from of it so that people from the block could admire the vehicle, shake your hand, and congratulate you on your acquisition.

Uncle Louie had a young man named Jimmy who worked for him in the store. I saw him every day. He had much to say about everything and was a Yankees fan in Brooklyn. He would tease me about how the Dodgers never won a World Series and other insults about the team that was second to the Yankees in New York City. Even as a young boy, I didn't think he was too intelligent so I didn't pay much attention to what he said. Almost thirty years later, I was managing a new acquisition of my company. I was having a casual conversation with one of the supervisors, Theresa. She lived in Brooklyn and we compared notes. When I told her where I had lived, she said that her husband was a partner in a dinette store there. After confirming that her husband was Jimmy, I realized that he had lied to his wife. He was only an employee of my uncle, never a partner. I did not burst any bubbles by revealing the truth. My father's words came back to me. "Always be yourself, you never know who you'll run into."

My parents had a group of friends that started out as five women from the PTA at my elementary school. One of the women was Aunt Lucy, married to Frank, one of my mother's brothers, so she and my mother had their feet in two camps. The men were all regular guys and the women were all neighborhood girls. Two of the men were sanitation workers, Uncle Frank was a welder at the Brooklyn Navy Yard, my father worked for the electric company, and the other was an elevator operator in what was then the RCA Building, later 30 Rock. Two of the women graduated high school and that was the extent of the group's level of formal education. They were close for several decades and only stopped their parties and travel as illness and death made their inevitable inroads.

All ten of the people were first generation Italian. They were funny and kind and were good friends from the time they met in Brooklyn to their final destinations after leaving the neighborhood. While they were all Italian, they were, like my parents, people with one foot in their old upbringing and the other in the newer world. They took a cruise together and went on frequent vacations to the Poconos. They had regular gatherings at each other's houses and always enjoyed the company of the others. One of the men had a reputation for being a lesser party animal than the rest of the crew. He caused my father and Uncle Frank to create a list of people who were considered dull. The joke was that all these people would go in one room on New Year's Eve. At midnight, they would stand up, clap once, and sit down. From that time until today, it is a family joke to assign people to "the room." Several people assign themselves to "the room" because they admittedly are not crazy about festivities of any kind. But most of the regular guys and girls looked forward to breaks from their daily lives, and to the good times in lives that started in poverty, lived through the Great Depression and World War II, dealt with loss, and now had modest comforts.

I thought the modest comfort was fine for these others but being American meant more than that to me. There must be, I hoped, a road out of the lives of those around me.

Chapter 7. The Church

God is everywhere, I was told. But to be with God, we had to go to church. "Is God there," I asked my mother, pointing to the door on the tabernacle on the altar. "Yes," she said, never being one to get deeply into religious mysteries.

Blessed Sacrament Church was an austere building, constructed around 1880 by the Germans who preceded the Italians into the neighborhood. The interior was of tan brick with a dome of the same substance, with little decor other than the usual cast of plaster saint statutes. My father always described it as "cold" in contrast to the sky blue and white motif of St. Anthony's, the church founded by the area's Italians in the early 1900s. St. Anthony's had paintings on the walls on the sides of the altar in the style of Renaissance and Baroque era churches in Italy. The statues of the saints were painted, all the better to see the blood and the wounds, and the eyes of St. Lucy on the plate she held.

Like many things in our lives, we did much by rote, because it was expected. Deviation was looked down upon. So, Sunday's was to dress nice for mass, then to a nearby bakery for warm Italian bread, the fluffy white kind, none of that grainy stuff that future generations saw as healthy, then the Sunday gravy, and that was the day, unless we went to the cemetery and to Aunt Rose's house later in the afternoon.

Blessed Sacrament was a few blocks closer but Mother preferred it for other reasons. Even though she was married in St. Anthony's and I was baptized there, she thought that church to be too Italian. She also had bad memories of her religious instruction there as a child. St. Anthony's had a school and a convent and its resident nuns who enforced the rules on the captive audience of kids in the school, which carried over to the public school children who went for lessons before receiving their first sacraments. The term wasn't used then but Blessed Sacrament was more "laid back," less strict, than the other church. Besides, they only had custody of the kids for an hour on Wednesday afternoon and for the children's mass and instructions afterwards on Sunday.

On the rare occasion when we went to Sunday mass at St. Anthony's due to schedule issues, I was very uncomfortable there. The sermon at the high mass was in Italian and too many of the people in attendance spoke Italian. My father grew up in this totally Italian enclave and, like my mother, preferred a more American venue. Mother confessed later that when she went to religious instructions in that school she was afraid of the nuns. Another reason why, perhaps, she opted for the non-Italian church when it was time to attend as an adult and to send me for the required and expected religious instructions.

In order to receive First Holy Communion, it was necessary to comply with a set of requirements. There was Released Time for religious instruction every Wednesday afternoon, plus more instruction on Sunday after the 9:00 a.m. children's mass.

With my usual companion at that age, cousin Vito, I attended my first children's mass at the beginning of first grade. For some reason, size order was a big thing in those days, since there was no concern about body shaming, stereotyping or hurting a kid's self esteem. Vito and I, therefore, were seated in the front row in the space closest to the aisle. There was no protective phalanx of other boys around us, no cushion for my shame of not knowing what to do. The mass was a series of kneeling, standing, prayers, and hymns. I didn't know the ritual at first and cried with discomfort and embarrassment. I hated being in an unfamiliar environment, in this case a church alone with other boys and girls and not with my mother.

I was a fast learner especially in this case where learning the ropes raised my comfort level. Learning the ropes and playing by the rules was one reason why I was successful in the eyes of adults, whether family, teachers, or nuns. A rebel I was not. So, I soon was familiar with what to do in response to each of the nuns' clicks, responses to whatever came from the altar and the words to the hymns. Likewise, I memorized the questions in the Catechism. We never read the Bible, just tracts where the questions and answers were provided so there was no room for interpretation: "Who made us?" "God made us." "Who is God? And so it went.

While cleaner than it was presented in Mel Gibson's "The Passion of the Christ," the crucifixion was a horrible and gruesome matter. Reminders were all around us. Statues of Jesus on the cross and the Stations of the Cross, fourteen vignettes of the whole process, were part of every church. The nuns read a passage "They have pierced my hands and my feet. They have numbered all my bones." Sister explained that Jesus was placed on the cross in a manner that showed his ribs and allowed them to be counted. My mother was in the church at the time and later tested me as to the meaning of that statement. It was too horrible for me to explain so I just said it was something about the cross. "You were looking around. You weren't paying attention," she said. I was paying attention but just found the explanation to be too grisly for me to repeat.

As the school year rolled on and the Wednesday and Sunday lessons educated us as to the mysteries of the universe, creation, heaven, purgatory, and hell, First Holy Communion was now a week away. As was drilled into us, to receive Communion, we had to be without sin. Thus, it was time for the sacrament of Confession. This was a scary thing but it made us feel that all other religions were easy because confession to a priest was not required. At seven years of age, I had not yet committed the sin that the priest in confession asked about, in detail, years later when he discerned my adolescent voice.

"Bless me Father, for I have sinned. This is my first Confession. These are my sins." There I was kneeling in the dark confessional, after thinking long and hard about what to confess. There was the nude picture of Marilyn Monroe on a calendar in my uncle's store, and a painting of a nude woman at the Brooklyn Museum of Art. OK, then, I looked at bad pictures. Maybe I missed mass once so I could say that. I was too young to have the "impure thoughts" that were big items as we grew up. I never ate meat on Friday since, like missing mass, this was a matter under my mother's control, not my own. So, it ended. I was given penance of five Hail Marys, said an Act of Contrition, and was ready to receive the Body and Blood of Jesus, and just as important, I was in a state of grace so if I died I would go straight to heaven.

There were numerous discussions and opinions about what to do if the host fell. Do we pick it up? But we are not supposed to touch the host. Do we just leave it where it fell? That can't be right. We never got official instructions from the nuns, probably because it was unlikely that the priest would miss our mouths when dispensing the host and there was the altar boy holding a plate under our chins in order to avoid such a disaster.

Finally, the big day came. The boys were in dark blue suits and the girls in white bride dresses. We marched in size order, Vito and I in the lead. It went without incident. There we were. One of the great rites of passage in our lives. After the mass, everyone was outside the church taking pictures. My father was big on home movies so he recorded us marching in, then hanging out afterwards, perfectly dressed as befitting our state of grace.

Since no eating was allowed before Communion, we were invited to the apartment of Vito's mother's sisters for breakfast. In the days before the Catholic Church relaxed its rules, a "Communion breakfast" was a big deal. Nothing Italian was on the menu, but there were bialys, bagels, and other fare that was available in a mixed neighborhood. Everything tasted great in light of what we had just achieved.

Since this was a big event, we then made the rounds to the homes of local family members who rewarded me with either a small sum of money, one dollar maximum, or some religious object, either a medal or small plastic statue, then to dinner in a nice restaurant. It was indeed a special day. Due to my state of grace, the religious artifacts in Aunt Rose's apartment were particularly appealing to me. They had a large crucifix on the wall with the Jesus figure in explicit detail. Aunt Rose was particularly enamored of the concave plaster depiction of Jesus' face. Due to the shape of this venerated object, his eyes followed you. "Isn't he handsome," she said of the blue eyed face with light brown hair. A decade later when many boys wore their hair long, family members would often say "He looks like Jesus Christ," although they were not being complimentary.

As an obedient son, student, and church goer, I strove to obey the rules exactly as set forth by the appropriate governing authority. The church had a great deal of such rules, some real, some made up by the other kids. For some reason, someone said we were not supposed to point in church. So I didn't point. The nuns said that when the priest raised the host, if we said "My Lord and my God," we got seven years off our time in purgatory. I wasn't sure how many years in purgatory I had earned but I figured that by losing seven years every Sunday and on holy days of obligation, I would accumulate a good number of Get Out of Jail Free cards.

"Mommy, I want to be an altar boy," I said one Sunday a few months after my First Communion. There was an announcement from the altar that slots were open. I found myself in the church's rectory with a group of other boys my age with an old priest in charge. The first thing we did was to read Latin from the books distributed. I could not read Latin and pronounced J's as J's and not as U's as it was done in Latin. I was in tears which was my usual reaction when I could not do something. My father was in the room and afterwards asked if I was reading on top of the words, which showed the phonetic pronunciation.

Ah, that was the solution. From then on, Latin was a breeze since I had good reading and memory skills.

Ad Deum qui laetificat juventutem meam. The Latin continued from there.

Unfortunately, the on the job training was poor and I found myself, once again, in a situation in which I was without experience or knowledge, and, therefore, mortified. As the low boy on the roster, I was assigned the 7:00 am weekday mass. Since I had no altar experience, I was supposed to assist one of the older boys, or even one of the men. My father took me before he went to work. There were four people in the church for mass at that hour. I entered the sacristy and put on the robes and waited for my mentor to arrive. He never did. "Father, I never served mass. Another boy was supposed to be here to teach me," I whimpered. "All right, just kneel and pray." He made some gestures to indicate when I should ring the bell when the host was consecrated but that was it. After the short mass was over, I quickly changed and found my father. I was in tears, yet another humiliating experience brought about by someone not being where they were supposed to be and doing what they were expected to do.

Gradually, my skills improved as I worked my way through the Latin ritual. I was too inexperienced to work weddings where I heard there were tips but it was all hands on deck for the novena, where we all lined up holding candles. Finally, I no longer felt like an outsider. Was that because there were few Italians in the altar boy crew so I felt I was among Americans?

My tenure did not last long. I did not enjoy the gig even as I became better at mastering all the steps of the ancient ritual. At eight years old, I guess I had not found my calling.

One of my definite callings was to be obedient and respect all authority. That served me well in school and seemed to work in life in general. There was a fund raising push to build Catholic high schools.

Even though my parents and I always attended public schools, I urged them to contribute to this drive. Why? Because the priest, from the altar, said we should. My parents were never ones to contribute to anything and certainly didn't have the funds for such things anyway, so no funding came from my family for Catholic high schools. "Charity begins at home." my father would say. In our circles, it did not mean that we should be kind to those close to us. It was an excuse not to give anything to anyone else, probably because no one could afford to give.

The church also had an event called "Mission Sunday." A priest from a mission in Asia or Latin America would speak from the altar to raise money for his mission. The stories told were quite nasty, usually about disease, starvation, and incredible poverty. One story was about a Catholic school in China after the Communists took over. The narrative was that the Communist soldiers said that the teacher was talking to a student about Jesus and the soldier cut out the teacher's tongue and stuck chopsticks in the student's ears. "She will never speak of that again and you will never hear it again," the soldier said. With stories like that, it was no surprise that when the mission basket was passed around, it was full of coins, and even some bills. "Daddy, if the Chinese are so bad, why don't we send the army and navy to fight them? We beat the Germans and the Japs, can't we beat the Red Chinese?" "China has a billion people and millions in their army. They don't care about life. In Korea, they sent human waves against us. They would do that again. We could bomb them but there are too many pinkos in the government who think we should get along with Russia and China even though they do such horrible things." I didn't like what I heard but knew my father was right.

I read, with fear and loathing, the articles in the *Brooklyn Tablet*, the newspaper of the diocese, about the evils of Russia and of communism. But the real reason to read that journal was to see the movie ratings by The Legion of Decency. The movies were categorized in bunches rated from "Morally Unobjectional for All" through various levels of being OK for adults, to the ultimate category of "Condemned." I was curious about what would make "Baby Doll" or "The Moon is Blue" too evil even for adults but as a child I figured the films must have had naked people. I had no idea at that time that a movie could have a story line that didn't promote Catholic and family values. The Catholic Church made a big deal of anything in popular culture that presented anything contrary to the accepted party line regarding sex, marriage, and family life. So, a movie did not have to be "dirty" to be condemned.

"Mom, at church today, we stood up to take a pledge that we would not see bad movies. Everyone stood up to take the pledge," I reported. It did not occur to me that we were too young to take a stand against censorship or to risk the consequences for not being part of the mass conformity.

My family was not into the detail parts of religion. It was mostly rote obligations and responses. We didn't have a Bible in the house. "Protestants are always quoting the Bible," my father would say, as if the book that was the basis of our religion was just a nuisance that should be ignored. Or perhaps, people were not playing fair by having actual knowledge of our religious origins. One of my father's brothers, Uncle Lorenzo, who everyone called "Larry", was regaling my father with some story about St. Paul that he picked up somewhere. "I know all about St. Paul," was my father's response. Of course, he knew nothing about St Paul other than that his name was associated with St. Peter.

"Daddy, did you hear about Our Lady of Fatima?" He didn't. I only knew because some kids who were better clued into what was happening in the Church told me about how the Blessed Virgin came to some children in Portugal and gave them a letter. The letter was supposed to be opened at midnight that began 1960. Speculation was that it would portend the end of the world.

I was allowed to stay up till midnight on New Year's Eve. Right at midnight, as the ball came down, and Guy Lombardo and this orchestra played "Auld Lang Sine," there was a breaking news bulletin on TV. "THEY OPENED THE LETTER," I shouted. In reality, the news was that a transit strike was averted.

Public school, a laid back church, and parents to whom religion was a convention, all led to a weak connection to the religion of my birth. We did enough to obey the basic rules. Church on Sundays, no meat on Friday or on Christmas Eve, making the sign of the cross when walking or driving past a church. My parents never went to confession or received Communion. As my mother would say, "I have nothing to confess." As I got older, I realized that many people had it much worse than my religious background of superficial gestures and technical obedience of the rules. But at that point in my life, I did not yet know families who had 7, 8, or 9 children because they took literally the Church's prohibition of birth control. Why more of those families were other than Italian did not occur to me then but looking back, it said a good deal about how Italian-Americans viewed our religion. Symbols and gestures were far more important than theology. I later learned that the more serious stuff, and thus the American hierarchy, was the property of the Irish.

Chapter 8. Our Un-American Traditions

"We are going to a very nice restaurant for Daddy's birthday," my mother told me. "Where are we going?" "Guy Lombardo's in Freeport. It is very exclusive." I didn't know exactly what "exclusive" meant but I figured this was going to be something special.

When the day came, we dressed in our best. My father wore a suit and tie, Jessica wore one of those scratchy fluffy dresses little girls were subjected to then, and I wore my red sport jacket. The place was near the water. It was not like any place I had been before. It was bright and airy with large windows with views of the canals and docks in that part of Long Island. What impressed me the most, however, was the genteel crowd. Jackets and ties for the men, dresses for the women, and the kids in their dress-up clothes. The staff treated Jessica and me as if we were special customers and offered us children's drinks—a Davy Crockett for me and a Shirley Temple for her. No booze of course, but with color that made them look like grownup cocktails and a maraschino cherry to tie the whole thing together. Is this what "exclusive" meant, I wondered?

Dad had a Manhattan, Mother had a hi ball. What occurred to me was that neither we, nor anyone I saw, had macaroni and gravy. Maybe some of the people were Italian, but to me, no one acted the way I expected Italians to act. The diners spoke in normal tones, and didn't look like my relatives. Did "exclusive" mean places where Italians didn't go?

In those days, such a place was special for us for several reasons. Of course, the high cost alone made it a very special place. Also, it was not an Italian restaurant. On the rare occasion that we ate out, we either went to a local Italian establishment or a generic place for hamburgers and sandwiches. Howard Johnson's for one. There were no fine restaurants in our local world and noses were turned up at anything ethnic like Chinese or a Jewish deli. I only went to Kishka King on Pitkin Avenue with cousin Loretta who was half Jewish. "American" was OK with me since I could get a hamburger and fries like a regular kid.

One of the strong traditions in our family was to criticize and minimize other ethnic groups. Blacks weren't even worthy of serious discussion regarding food or culture. Much was said, however, about Jews.

"Jewish ladies like to get all dressed up with makeup and jewelry," according to my father, "but they don't care about their house. They don't care if the house is messy as long as they get all dolled up." "Rhoda's house is clean," Mother replied. "That's because she learned from you," was my father's spin.

A frequent subject was how Jewish women didn't care about their kids. "They send them to camp because they want to get rid of them," according to Mother. Later, I heard the same theme when it was time for college. According to Mother, going away to college was the chance to free the mothers of their offspring so they could shop at Fortunoff's or something. Sending your kid to a commuter college showed love, while also making sure they were home at a reasonable hour to prevent your kid from having sex. The fact that several cousins either were pregnant out of wedlock or got a girl in trouble, none of whom went to college was not in keeping with her worldview and, therefore, ignored.

While some of the more extreme views were modified as mother and father expanded their horizons from the neighborhood, it was always part of their mindset that Italians were superior in our culture, food, and lifestyles, especially our food. Even among Italians, they had things to say about Sicilians for example. "Sicilians, they are always jealous of each other. If one has a new piece of jewelry, the other has to have it too." "He is a real *Calabraise,* " Mother once said, meaning that the person whose origins were in Calabria was stubborn and "hard headed."

Of course, not all traditions involved superiority over anyone who wasn't from a region of Italy between Naples and Sicily, we had plenty of other things to cling to.

"Ma, we're Americans, why do you talk Italian?" My parents spoke English well but grew up in households where Italian was spoken since their parents were all born in Italy. They really only spoke Italian when they didn't want us kids to understand. So, there were Italian phrases that indicated that there were a lot of black people in the area, that someone was unattractive, or that a woman either was, or looked like, a slut. I never was able to distinguish between the appearance, or actuality, of a woman's moral standing since all I knew about the word *putana* was that it meant a bad girl. Nor did I know what actually made a girl bad when I was still in my single digits.

I knew a number of Italian words gleaned from family usage, but I didn't know till much later that my family mispronounced words using the dialect from the south of Italy. For one thing, vowels at the end of words were usually dropped, and the letter c was pronounced as a g. That gave us *gabagool* for capicola, *manigut* for manicotti, and *madenade* for marinara. What made it even worse was that the family made fun of someone who pronounced a word correctly from a menu because they weren't connected to the actual way we spoke. "That woman over there ordered ma ri nara," my father would say, using an exaggerated pronunciation as a means of ridiculing a person so clueless that she used the word properly.

Uncle Fred's favorite word was "gitdrool," meaning a person with limited intelligence and a poor personality. Mother told me that the word meant "cucumber" a fitting appellation for a person with the aforementioned personality traits. It turned out that the actual word for cucumber is *cetriolo*. Not even close.

If they were going to use Italian words, at least they could use the right words, I thought. I gradually learned how my family and the others in the neighborhood spoke a low-class kind of Italian. I had not ventured into those areas of society where my Italian background was irrelevant but had a vague sense that there were places and people that used language correctly, not interlaced with Italian words or with the Brooklyn accent everyone spoke. The place where the sidewalk met the street was the "curve." You put "earl" in the car, and "dem," "dees," and "dose," were actually spoken outside of Bowery Boys movies. Mother spoke proper English hoping to transition from the old world of immigrants and their children to the new one that was a few steps away.

"My mother and I used to go to the Italian theater," Mother announced in connection with nothing in particular. "They did plays in Italian and Momma used to cry. They were always about missing their families who were still in Italy or about children being mean to their parents. We went to the Majestic Theater on Fulton Street and sometimes to the Brooklyn Academy of Music. My mother loved Mario Badalati who was soooo handsome. We also saw Gilda Mignoetti, who sang Italian songs. I didn't care for that music but liked to go anywhere with my mother. I liked American singers like Frank Sinatra and big band music. Daddy and I loved to dance to the Tommy Dorsey Orchestra or to Glenn Miller."

The subject of the Italian theater came up again many years later when I was at home and Vincent Gardenia was on some sitcom in TV. "I used to see him in the Italian theater with his father, Gennaro Gardenia. They did a play where the father was a hard-working laborer in America and he put his son through law school. The son became a successful lawyer. He was at a fancy party and his father was looking for him because he needed his son's help. The son pretended he didn't know him and told him to go away because he was badly dressed. 'Go away, you dirty old man. This is no place for you.' Momma got so mad. People in the audience were yelling at the stage. How could a son treat his father that way after all he did for him?"

I told her that there were similar themes in the Yiddish theater, about losing your child in the new world. "No," Mother relied, "he was ashamed of this father." "Sure, that is what happened on the stage, but the real theme was the fear of their children being assimilated, becoming American." "He was ashamed of his father," was her reply. At that point I dropped the subject understanding that she would not get beyond the literal to understand the deeper meaning as to why such plays were written by immigrants. That in breaking tradition, a young person becomes more distant from the old country and all that means. Success did not just mean a different life just the same life just with a bigger house and a better car. As she said years later, with anticipated pride, "When you are a big-shot lawyer, you're gonna drive by in your Cadillac and honk on your way home to your big house in Great Neck."

Some traditions were common among my family and the families of my Italian friends but they may not have been Italian traditions. "The party's in the kitchen," Vito's aunts would say at his birthday party in his railroad apartment. They had a big kitchen that was unusually large for that neighborhood, so all activity took place there, even a kid's birthday party. What that meant was stay out of the living room. That room was small and contained all the "good" furniture." So, therefore, there was a gate to keep kids out.

Another means by which people kept their furniture from actually being used was to cover fabric with plastic slipcovers. Slippery when cold, sticky when hot, and always uncomfortable, nothing said working class more than plastic slip covers. In the journey from working class to lower middle class, women tried hard to keep things "nice" without realizing that these attempts to preserve their treasures said more about class than they realized. "Ma, how come we have this plastic? Nobody on television has them." "I want to keep the couch and the chairs nice and clean," was the reply. In later years, when we moved to our house in the suburbs, the preservation efforts were perfected. In addition to covering the furniture, beautiful hardwood floors were covered by carpeting, known as "broadloom." This prevented scuffs, scratches and indentations make by overweight women in spike heels. An extra level of protection was added via plastic runners in the more heavily traveled areas, such as that leading to the doors.

Was this an Italian-American tradition? It seemed like it to me then. Looking back, I realized that these were people who grew up poor, lived through the Great Depression, and treated their possessions as treasures. "Good" furniture cost money, and there were not the resources for replacements, so these had to be preserved, by keeping them new. So much of their lives was to show off their houses as a sign of success as Americans that they could not risk the wear and tare of everyday use.

One day, my mother showed me a dollar bill where one side was upside down from the other. As a patriotic American, I thought that this bill was counterfeit and should immediately be turned in to the government. "I am not giving up a dollar." was her reply. Several thoughts came to me years later. The first, of course, was that no one would bother producing counterfeit one dollar bills. The other was that such a printing anomaly would make that bill valuable to a collector. Yet, the real takeaway was that funds were so tight that all she thought of was that she would not give up a dollar.

"Brian, on Sunday, we are going to eat at my cousin Mary's house," Millie proclaimed one night at dinner. "I never heard of her. Does she have children?" "Well, she isn't my first cousin like you and Vito. My mother and her mother were cousins. Her children are grown up. She has a son in the army and a daughter who is nineteen, I think, who lives with them. You have to get dressed up nice because it's a Sunday." I wondered why she said that since I always dressed up nice on Sunday, first for church, then for whatever else we did, usually a visit to Aunt Rose, or a visit from Aunt Rose.

On that Sunday, we took a long drive through unfamiliar areas of the city, across the Triborough Bridge and into the Bronx. I had never been to the Bronx, except one visit to the zoo. The neighborhood was obviously Italian, much more so than in my corner of Brooklyn. There was a large Catholic church on the corner, with a school on the grounds, and what Mother explained was a convent, a place where nuns lived. Since our church had neither, I recognized that this was a territory unlike what I was used to. The stores and restaurants were all Italian, with neon signs proclaiming pizza, or names like Villa Napoli, and Minucci's. The grocery stores had dried sausages in the windows, along with hanging provolone, and displays of olive oil. "Millie," my father said. " Do you want to buy anything here? They got some nice stuff." "Nah, I can get what I want from my own stores."

Our destination was a small private house, on a block that was a mix of small apartment buildings, attached row houses, and detached houses that shared a driveway with the house next door and had a small patch of grass in the front. There was a statue of the Virgin Mary in a concave plaster setting painted blue on the inside. "They are very religious," Mother said, as if she felt she needed to warn me of what to expect. At eight years old, I bought into religious conventions but I was not prepared for what I saw inside.

The house was decorated for Christmas which was only two weeks away, but the decorations went beyond anything I had seen in someone's house. The Nativity scene was not in an accustomed place under the tree. It was on a side table in the living room. The figures were six inches or so in height and consisted of more than the usual baby Jesus in the manger, Mary and Joseph, a cow and a donkey and the Three Wise Men. There were also five or six shepherds along with their sheep and other figures that I could not identify. I asked who they were and Mary told me that they were people who came to witness the birth of Our Lord.

The walls were covered with pictures of various saints, some of which portrayed their martyrdom. There was one of St. Lawrence on a grate over a fire where he was roasted alive and St. Sebastian with numerous protruding arrows, along with St. Francis receiving Jesus' wounds. Less gruesome was a print of Jesus ascending into heaven and others of various cathedrals around the world. I was fascinated by Mary's piety and wondered if this was the level of devotion needed to get to heaven. If that was the case, my family might be in trouble.

We sat down to a dinner that was the usual Sunday fare, first meatballs and sausages and spaghetti, then roast beef, potatoes and carrots. I remember the meal being pretty good, considering how fussy I was about the gravy, whether it had skin, chunks and seeds from the tomatoes. In fact, the sauce was smooth and absent the unwelcome yuck. Everyone complimented the bread, which varied from neighborhood to neighborhood and signified the host's ability to deliver something special from local sources.

What was most memorable about the dinner was the conversation dominated by Mary. She obviously was active in the church judging from her interminable quotes from the parish priest. "Father said that you should only send your kids to Catholic schools because public schools are run by Jews and Communists." My father responded, not by arguing about the evils of such bigotry but by saying how my school was a good one, that we started each day with the Pledge of Allegiance and that most of the teachers in the school were not Jewish. "I went to that school and I am in PTA now and I am there all the time. Nobody is teaching the kids that communism is a good thing," was Mother's response.

Mary then pivoted to what the priest said about Joe McCarthy. "Father said he died of a broken heart because he saw what is happening with Communists taking over America." Father also was opposed to plans to build a bridge between Brooklyn and Staten Island because the Russians could bomb the bridge and make it collapse so navy ships won't be able to get out of the Brooklyn Navy Yard. At my young age, as an avid cold warrior, that sounded reasonable to me.

Having said all she had to say about global issues, Mary then brought it down to the personal, "Did you hear that Florence's daughter moved out? After she graduated high school, she got a job in an office in the city. She got an apartment in Greenwich Village. She said she wanted to be closer to work." Everyone agreed that it was a scandal and even a sin for a girl to get her own place before she got married. Mary's husband, Frank, finally got a word in. "A girl gotta get married from the house. Only tramps and beatniks get their own apartments. She thinks who she is because she graduated high school." Their daughter Anne finally spoke up about something, obviously intimidated by her parent's strong opinions on all subjects. "I don't see what's wrong with a girl having her own apartment." Mary's kind and understanding reply was "Why don't you just shut up? You want to live with the beatniks, go head. If you think we will pay for your wedding, you got another thing coming."

At my age, I had no opinion about girls moving out before they were married. I had no idea of the underlying fear of their parents that they may have sex, get pregnant, and ruin the family's reputation. Yes, it was a tradition to protect a girl's virtue so they would remain marriage material. Otherwise, they would be the parent's responsibility forever. Who ever heard of an Italian girl being self sufficient and not dependent on her father or her husband?

Chapter 9. The Cold Warrior

"Could we beat Russia in a war? " I asked my father. "We have Russia surrounded. We got bases in Europe, Turkey, Japan, and all over the Pacific. They got a bigger army but we have a bigger navy."

I don't specifically recall what triggered my concern about Russia by the time I was seven years old, but like most good Americans, I saw Russia as the enemy. During one of our trips to the Brooklyn Navy Yard, we heard a lecture by Navy brass, accompanied by film strips, explaining why we need a big navy in the era of atom bombs, missiles and jet planes. The film strip showed the Eurasian land mass with the vast areas of Eastern Europe, the Soviet Union, and China, covered in red. This is what the United States is up against, according to our host. Progressing though the film strip, there was a graphic of about 400 submarine symbols, which was the Soviet fleet that could threaten to cut off our oil supply from the Arab countries and South America. The next strip was of 37 subs, which is what Nazi Germany had at the start of WWII and caused so many shipping losses. A large navy, therefore, was essential to contain this clear and present danger. I didn't need more convincing.

The first news I was aware of outside of baseball were several events in 1956. Dwight Eisenhower, to that point the only president I knew, was running for reelection. It seemed unpatriotic for anyone to run against him. When I heard from some kid on the block that Adlai Stevenson, his opponent, wanted school on Saturday, that really sealed the deal for me. I was greatly relieved when I learned that Ike won in a landslide.

There always seemed to be a radio on somewhere, in our car, my uncle's store, or in our kitchen. I kept hearing the term "Hungarian refugees." I asked what that was about and Mother explained that Russia invaded Hungary and a lot of people left the country. Dad said that Russia kept its army in Eastern Europe after "the war." When the people of Hungary tried to kick out the Russians, they came back with tanks and artillery and killed people. "That's why we have to have a big army and navy. Russia is really dangerous. If we didn't have ships and troops in Europe, they would take over France and England and attack us next." "We can beat them, right?" I asked. "We could beat them in a war, but there are too many pinkos in the government who don't think we should be tough on Russia. They could take over this country without firing a shot."

There were times, however, when my anxiety over Russia was assuaged. An air show at Mitchell Field on Long Island was one of those times. Seeing large transports lined up with their propellers revving, knowing that they could transport thousands of our boys, along with hundreds of tanks, anywhere the Russians threatened, boosted my confidence. Nothing compared, however, to the trips to the Brooklyn Navy Yard. Vito and I, along with our fathers, got to walk on the deck of the newest aircraft carrier, the Saratoga. We were told how many football fields could fit on the flight deck and how many jets the ship could hold. "Russia don't have any carriers, right, Dad?" I asked. They don't, he answered but they have more subs than we do, a fact borne out that same day by the naval officer's talk and film strip.

The entire county, not just me, was shocked and frightened when we learned that Russia put a satellite into space. Sputnik worries permeated the news and discussions. "Russia is ahead of us in missiles," my father said. That statement was backed up by one failure after another of attempts to launch an American satellite. Fears abounded that if they could put a satellite into space, they could put a bomb into space, and that they had the missiles powerful enough to reach our homeland. In response, schools upped their programs in science and math so we could "catch up" to Russia.

"In Russia, they train everyone to be engineers. In this country, they go to college and study poetry. No wonder they are ahead of us," was my father's take on the situation. I didn't know what an engineer actually did but knew that I wanted to be one. I owed that to my country. Mother, through her experience in the Navy Department, said I could go to college to become an engineer and then become an officer in the navy. At that point in my life the significance to her of being a navy officer was not yet known to me. She used the expression "an officer and a gentleman" which seemed to be the right fit for someone with my intelligence and lofty standards.

I didn't want to sit back at let the Russians have their way with us so I proposed some steps I could take to protect America. I designed a missile. The nose cone had a plunger that, when the missile hit the ground, would push into the payload and detonate the bomb. As I explained, "You get the missile over Russia, and when it hits the ground this part goes in and makes the bomb blow up," I proudly explained to anyone in my vicinity. My father put a kibosh on my invention when he said that is sort of how things are made to explode and the hard part is getting a missile from here to get over a target. Disappointed by not defeated, I had another plan. "We could build a small boat and go in the water near the airport with binoculars and look for Russian planes and warn the Air Force if we see any." Again, my father hit me with a reality check. "We have radar all over the world and planes patrolling at all times. If Russian planes came, we would know if before we would see them near the airport," was his logical explanation. I then made a list of all the countries that would side with us and would side with Russia if we had a war. The list included every country I could think of whether or not they were actually allied with either side of the cold war. As part of my military strategy, I suggested to cousin Vito that we should build "fifty atomic-powered battleships" since there were by then fifty states and battleships were named after states. I had no idea of budgets and figured the government could just build whatever it wanted. I did not consider that no battleships had been built since WWII and even during the height of that war, we never had fifty. I was very concerned about how the United States was to handle the Russian threat. Whoever pushed the fear agenda in those days certainly was successful with me. I was somewhat comforted by the model aircraft on the mobile hanging over my bed. I knew that whatever the Russians started, we had our F-104s, B-58s, and the other aircraft designed to intercept intruding planes, bomb targets, take off from carriers, and to perform whatever missions they were designed for.

The whole society was mobilized against the Russian threat. There were occasional air raid drills where sirens went off and everyone was supposed to shelter. In school, we went into the halls, crouched down facing the walls, and put our hands over our heads. I thought that if the Russians attacked, they would use WWII style attacks with conventional bombs. At the time, it didn't dawn on me that any attack would be with nuclear weapons or "atom bombs" as we called them. What chance would we have had if they dropped "big one?" Right after one such drill, a family friend came upstairs to say hello to my mother. They were talking about what was being broadcast about the potential holocaust. The fact that a missile could reach New York from Russia in twenty minutes was information too scary to digest.

It was a few years later that the threat from Russia was to me a battle between communism and "freedom." For the time being, for me, Russia was bad and that was all I needed to know.

Chapter 10. Leaving for the Promised Land

During the summer of 1959, Bobby Darin's hit version of *Mack the Knife* was played constantly on the radio, which was ever present in the days before ear plugs and personal music. I hummed that tune and tears flowed. Not because the song had any particular meaning to me but because I was sad, lonely, and felt that I had nothing to look forward to. At age 9, I was depressed. The slightest thing made me cry. Nothing gave me pleasure. A song about an anniversary with the line "here's to days gone by," made me choke back tears.

My gloomy feelings started in mid summer when the signs about driving carefully, school is open, and TV commercials about all the great products to make school life wonderful, began to appear.

"Brian is upset about going back to school. I don't know what to do. He is always crying. He doesn't eat. He was never like this before," my mother explained to one of her friends from the PTA. "Why should he feel that way? He is such a good student," was the obvious response. It was true. I was the best student in my class, popular with the other kids, never bullied, and even chatty with the principal, Mr. Levine, due to my high status in my grade, and my mother's active participation in school affairs through the PTA.

Apart from cousin Vito, my best friend was Robert D. He had been in my class since we started kindergarten and lived across the street. His family had the ground floor of the house which meant he had use of the backyard and the basement. The backyard had a small pool which was unusual in that neighborhood. The basement consisted of several railroad rooms with a clear view to each through the doorway. Robert was a fan of archery so a target was set up on one end of the basement. I learned to use a bow and arrow and eventually had one of my own, of limited strength but enough to hone my skills.

Robert was a good student so we could spend time talking about things beyond who could take who in a fight. He was very proud of his spelling ability and was one of the best students in our class. During the spring of fourth grade he was one of the ten of us selected to take a test. The test lasted over three complete school days. We didn't know what the test was for or what the results were and thought no more about it.

Rare in the neighborhood of Catholics, Jews, and Baptists, his family were Pentecostal Protestants. In the days when religion mattered to me, we discussed that was similar and what was different about our faiths. We agreed that we were all followers of Christ but his church did not have the rituals and symbols that the Catholic Church did. No holy water, statues, or confession. That was not a barrier between us since he was always friendly, never a "wise guy" and always around to play whatever street game was going on.

One day, he told me that he wasn't going to be with me in fifth grade. His family was moving to Long Island. That struck me hard. I knew that others were leaving the neighborhood, some to places as close as Ozone Park but his leaving combined with what seemed like an exodus, left me with an empty feeling. Cousin Vito was still nearby, my uncle's store downstairs was still in business, and he and his family still lived just across the street, but I was sensing that my world was changing. The neighborhood was increasingly African American, or "colored" using the more polite of the words in use at the time. I no longer heard of any white families moving in. The Dodgers were gone for two seasons. I knew Brooklyn was no longer the place for me.

Going into fifth grade, I was only two years away for the junior high that was two blocks away. Among kids, there was always talk of what the older kids did to the new students. I was told I would not go there anyway since I would qualify for "SP", the Special Progress school where students did three years of junior high in two. For some reason, the City of New York had several programs so that the better students could graduate at a younger age, for a purpose that has always escaped me.

My father was very understanding and we would have long talks that would ease my depression for awhile, but it would come back. He said school is at the same place I have always gone, with the same kids and the subjects would not be harder than before, and besides, I was the best student in my class. Looking back, I know that returning to school was just a trigger for all the fears, anxiety, melancholy, and separation anxiety I felt. What would it be like when my parents got old? Would I have to leave my home to go to college? What would I be when I grew up?

The big day came, the dreaded first day of school. When I entered the class, and saw my regular school mates, the lump in my throat began to loosen. The teacher was a very nice woman and I resumed my place as the prized pupil. Just as the cloud was beginning to break up, Mr. Levine called my mother and me into his office.

Meanwhile, my family spent the summer of my depression and the beginning weeks of the school year looking at houses on Long Island. We seemed to look to Long Island for everything. We went to Jones Beach and no longer Rockaway Beach. We drove to one of the closer towns to go to the drive-in movie. Car trips invariably were to the east, exploring the Long Island landscape, focusing on the areas in the middle of Nassau County that were filled with thousands of recently built track houses. We clearly were not interested in the pre-war houses in the older parts of the towns.

I desperately wanted to move. For one thing, friends and acquaintances were moving and I was feeling left behind. Also, I believed that as a real American, I should live in a house, surrounded by grass, and wooded areas to explore, not in a railroad apartment above my uncle's store. My father's income was not large and, like most women with children in that era, my mother stayed at home. Even then I understood some of the realities of real estate. The closer to the city the suburban town was, the more expensive it was. So the journey was incrementally longer each trip to the promised land.

At that stage of my life, any suburban house looked good to me. I didn't realize that there were some areas that were more upscale than others although the word "upscale" wasn't used then. We didn't look in North Shore towns like Manhasset or Great Neck. Our vista was in the middle of the island, not near the shore areas that were pricier. While I thought it would be great to live in a house with an upstairs so, perhaps, I could have a space apart from my parents if friends were over, my mom was set on a ranch. "I don't want to go up and down stairs all day when I clean the house and make the beds," Mother would say. Even after we moved, she was never impressed by a colonial, no matter how beautiful. She was only attracted to ranch houses.

We found our perfect house. It was a small ranch in South Farmingdale, a lower middle class community where a large number of the men worked for Grumman and Republic Aviation, or for their subcontractors. The cold war was in full swing and the country was producing jets and other aircraft at practically a wartime pace. Very few adults had a college degree and there were many Italian Americans in the community. In short, a perfect place for us.

Since every silver lining in my life came with a cloud, there was a big one here. My mother's family collectively owned the house where we lived and where Uncle Louie had his store. If we moved, only Uncle Louie would benefit from the property. The family wanted to sell the house. Since they were Italian, they didn't want to sell to someone who wanted the store area and would evict Uncle Louie. It was decided that Uncle Louie would buy out his siblings. It was a reasonable solution that would allow all the brothers and sisters to benefit from a house that had been in the family for thirty years, where they all grew up.

When the time came to complete the arrangement, Uncle Louie said "Are you kidding?" No excuse, no explanation, no apology. While the rest of the family could have used the money, we had those dollars specifically earmarked for the down payment for that little ranch house in South Farmingdale. I was a worrier and was always listening for what was going on around me, especially in my house, and especially when a matter affected me personally. Without that money, it appeared to be impossible to afford that house, to leave my shabby neighborhood for the green environs of Long Island, where real Americans lived in private houses, with lawns, and where I could play baseball all day with other white kids in the vast fields that surrounded the schools. My anxiety and depression was not helped by this sudden blow. It didn't help that almost every weekend we drove to look at the model house in the town where I so badly wanted to live.

I noticed that my mother was sadder than usual but my father was deeply disturbed. He knew how much mother and I wanted to move and obviously was distressed by his inability to make that happen. Years later I learned that he roughed up Uncle Louie for reneging on his promise that meant so much to us. Year's later, Uncle Louie spun the story that his family tried to throw him out of his store. In reality, as the landlord, the store would have been his. He won the battle, keeping the store at some very low rent until he bought it for almost nothing many years later. No remorse, no explanation.

Mr. Levine knew my mother because she was active in the PTA. He knew me through my mother and because I was the top student. I had spent a good deal of time in his office but not for disciplinary purposes. He would quiz me with mental puzzles and we would discuss various things about current events or whatever came to mind. I felt comfortable in his office.

The day he asked my mother and me to see him turned out to be a key moment in my life. "Brian, you did so well in the tests you took in the spring that you are going to be skipped to 6th grade." I was stung.

I was gradually getting over the reentry depression and anxiety over entering 5th grade and now this? Do I ever get a break? I summoned the courage to go against the command of the authority figure and said "I don't want to be skipped. Why can't I stay in my class? All my friends are in that class." The reply from Mr. Levine was "You will be bored."

In those days, most parents considered school authorities as the last word in matters regarding education, discipline, and behavior. I told my parents that I did not want to be skipped but they did not want to counter the directive of Mr. Levine. In the midst of my anxiety about my desire to move, and about school and life in general, I did not need the added trauma of a new class, and with older students as well.

Mr. Levine's "solution" to my reticence was that I should try the new class. If I didn't like it, I could go back. At the time, I didn't know what the impact would be for me to be the youngest in my class throughout puberty and adolescence, and in a new school in a new town. So I made the move. There was nothing not to like about my new class. The teacher was one I had in third grade. The format was the same. One teacher, one class, no changing of classes for different subjects. I stayed.

Meanwhile, we made constant trips to see the model house of the one to be built on a lot on a quiet street in South Farmingdale. The loss of the money from the sale of our current house due to my uncle's backing out of the deal, made it less likely that we would buy the house, and more likely that we would stay in Brooklyn, away from the suburban paradise where typical Americans lived. The trip from Brooklyn passed miles of houses along the Southern State Parkway, as well as beautiful new schools. Everything good seemed to be happening on Long Island while our neighborhood in Brooklyn was getting worse. There was no new construction, the schools were old, we heard of more muggings and gangs, and our people were moving away. "The sermon at the high mass at Saint Anthony's is in Spanish," my father pronounced one day. "That means this is a portarican neighborhood now. The sermon used to be in Italian." "What are you gonna do," my mother replied. "They are taking over. I rather have portaricans than coloreds," mother elaborated. "At least they are Catholic, not those holly rollers or whatever they are in those churches in the stores." Then, in a whispered aside that, of course, I heard, she said "Pete, we gotta get outta here."

As what happens often in life, events put things in a different perspective and make decisions for you. My father had the day off and walked Jessica to school. In the school yards where the lower grades lined up with their partners before entering the classroom, Jessica's partner was a Black boy. "Jessica was holding hands with a colored boy," my father reported. "That's it, we're gonna move."

That was the proverbial straw. Regardless of the lack of the wished for and expected funds from the sale of our house, he was now determined to leave. After heavy negotiations with the savings and loan component of his company, they were finally granted a mortgage. The contract was signed and the closing happened. That was the first time I heard the term "closing" in that context but I knew our dream house was now ours.

We were all excited about the new house. While it was a modest, three-bedroom ranch, it was well appointed. There was a large bathroom, a roomy, eat-in kitchen with a good deal of counter space and numerous hardwood cabinets. My parents did boring grownup things like lining the cabinets, measuring the windows for blinds, and planning on new furniture. I was to keep my bedroom set but Jessica would get a new set of real furniture. The living room and dining area were to be in "Danish Modern" style, clean lines with lots of orange and brown.

I wanted to bring something of my own before we actually moved in so I delivered my plastic model of Babe Ruth and placed it on the window sill since there was not yet any furniture. I was excited about the basement, which was the same size as the upstairs. My parents said they would "finish" the basement. A finished basement was a must so that kids could play with their friends without messing up the good furniture upstairs and for family gatherings which were frequent in those days and well populated. That project wasn't immediate due to time and costs constraints but I knew it was on the horizon since my parents seemed to have everything well planned.

Meanwhile, I heard my mother tell people that we would move in May. This reignited my anxiety. How could we move before the school year ended and I graduated? How could I start a new school with only six weeks or so to go? Every time I heard the word "May" my eyes welled up and my throat closed. Spring of the 6th grade was actually a pleasant time for me. I was well established in my new grade, and doing well. We also seemed to have no academic program left. We spent most of our time rehearsing folk dances for the May Day festival in Prospect Park. "I'm Captain Jinx of the Horse Marines; I feed my horse with corn and beans..."

But the weeks passed and it looked like the move would be pushed back until after graduation. We received our autograph books and signed greetings and sentiments to each other. Writings from people outside the school were also acceptable. And we had a "prom," a small dance in the school basement where parents supplied simple food and drinks and we danced to the latest rock and roll songs--sung by Ricky Nelson or Connie Francis. In short, all the trappings of moving on, drilled down commensurate with the fact that this was only elementary school.

On the big day, we gathered in the auditorium on the top floor of my 1892 school for observances and awards. The very last award and I guess the highest went to one girl, my friend Elizabeth, and one boy, me!

The parents went home and we finished our last day of elementary school. For me it was the last day of school in the City. Mother saw me as I approached the house in my jacket and tie, holding my medal. When I entered our apartment, she burst into tears. Her little boy was moving on and we were moving out. We were moving from the house where she grew up, where she raised Jessica and me, where she nursed her mother when she was dying of cancer, where her brother's store was downstairs, where that brother and her nieces lived across the street, where another brother lived one block away, where another lived four blocks away, where she went to the same elementary school I did, where the family gathered for so many occasions on the garage roof, and where it was the only home she knew.

A few days later, movers came and put our furniture in their truck. We got in our car and headed east. This time it was not to look at houses, but to live in one. I was about to become a real American. I was going to live in a house of our own. There would be no elderly Italians upstairs, no dinette store downstairs where people gathered. We would have a lawn. We would have a backyard. There was a drainage ditch down the street with trees on both sides. That was the "creek." There were woods along the parkway with a bicycle path that led to the "lake," the pond where the street waters from the creek ended up. And there was "town" with Main Street.

For a ten-year old boy, this was the American dream.

Epilogue The Promise Fulfilled?

A new world opened for me at ten-years old. The house was new. The living room and dining area furniture was new. The grass was beginning to grow. My new life seemed bright and I was excited and optimistic about my status as a real American.

The summer was a bit lonely. Jessica connected with the two girls next door who were around her age. The boy on the other side of our house was a bit younger than me but old enough to play catch and talk about baseball. Most of the summer, however, was spent alone. I did not yet have school friends and there weren't many kids around during the day. I read a lot of books and waited each month for the new issue of *Mad* and each day for the afternoon paper so I could see the results of the Dodgers game on the West Coast. Even though the team now played in Los Angeles, I was still a fan since players from Brooklyn, notably my idol, Duke Snider, were on the team.

Still, I felt like a real American kid because I could walk to the "creek" or take the bicycle path through the woods on the side of the parkway to the creek's terminus, the lake. It was only a pond that collected the rain water from the streets but in contrast to my old neighborhood, the ride there seemed like a bucolic adventure.

Farmingdale had Main Street, where there was a library, stores, eateries, and a movie theater. This was going to "town." There was even an ice cream parlor which I equated with the malt shop where Ozzie Nelson and his boys hung out.

Before school started, I was tested and placed into the honors class of the seventh grade. Our grade was the highest in the elementary school. We had a separate wing so I never saw the lower grade kids. The school was only a few years old and seemed perfect and modern compared to my last school. I tried hard to be upbeat about everything, the school's facilities, and even the lunch menu which, for twenty-five cents provided for hamburgers, pizza, ravioli, "barbecued beef on a buttered bun" and other delights, along with various side dishes. If the day's offerings didn't appeal, there was always the soup and sandwich option.

When classes finally started, I learned that my course of study included Latin and French and a different class and teacher for each subject. This was a big change from Brooklyn where I had one teacher in the same class all day for all subjects. Because I started school earlier than I should have and skipped fifth grade, I was only ten while my classmates were turning twelve as the school year progressed. Since this was the honors class, due to the age difference and a course of study well beyond anything I had experienced, I was no longer the top student. I struggled at first until, eventually, I found my pace and held my own. My entry into this new and challenging environment was not helped by a sadistic English teacher who took every opportunity to humiliate me for minor errors and gaffes. There was a conference with my parents, this teacher, the principal, and my homeroom teacher, who also taught the Latin and French classes. The English teacher recommended that I be put back into sixth grade. I wasn't at the meeting but learned that my mother laid into her for her tactics of ridicule and intimidation. The homeroom teacher was also on my side, according to my parents. After that, I was no longer the victim of abuse and my grades jumped after that first marking period. This was, however, the first time I was subjected to any negative action in school. It passed but let me know that I was no longer on the top of the heap.

After a few weeks at my new school, I began to realize that my new town was not the perfect paradise I had envisioned. I had believed that suburbanites were affluent, educated people. How else could they afford to buy a house? My town was filled with refugees from working class areas of Brooklyn who brought their prejudices with them. One of the great fears was that someone would sell a house to "coloreds" thus ruining the town. There was frequent opposition to the school and library budgets because they were not strong supporters of education. They felt they did fine in their blue collar jobs and, also, were on tight budgets so any tax increases were met with hostility. Still, there was a cadre of people who supported the schools and the library so, in fact, there was more than one camp in my town.

As a young kid, I learned that my classmates in the honor's class or team mates on my Little League teams were not the only kids my age. There were many kids we called "hoods." They were usually poor students, not active in school or community activities, and managed to make life miserable for the rest of us. They always traveled in packs so it became necessary to avoid certain locations for fear of being harassed. A frequent hangout for these boys was the little foot bridge over the creek. That could not be avoided when walking to and from school. Often several of them, always at least three, usually more, would stand there and hassle me, "What's your name? You got hairy balls?" were a few examples of the intelligent repartee from them. Unlike the Fonz, or the characters in *Grease,* they were not at all amusing or good natured. Later, in high school, the atmosphere changed for the better when the new principal expelled a number of these lads.

Still, I mostly prospered. By high school, I caught up to the best students, and became one myself. I was active in school politics and a member of the Key Club, which was a selective boys' organization at the time. I met my wife in high school although we didn't start dating until after I had graduated while she was still there. My father kept our house for fifty years so I constantly visited the house and the town. My daughters loved to play in the backyard or in the basement. We visited on holidays, for dinners at home, or out in restaurants, for cook outs for Father's Day and summer birthdays, until my father passed away.

Farmingdale has always been my home town. High school, family holidays, meeting my wife, years of visits, continued even after my mother's passing many years before my father. Of course, as an adult, I changed my concept of what it meant to be American. It was more than being white and living in a small town in a house surrounded by grass.

My mother and I often talked about our pasts, where we came from, and where we wanted to go. One day, she was reminiscing about various people and events in her life while my daughters were playing in the inflatable pool my father set up when his grand children visited in the summer. For some reason, she talked about her time in the Navy Department during World War II. She remembered how refined the people were, how different from her neighborhood in Brooklyn. In many ways, this experience led to her aspirations to a middle class suburban life and to college education for her son and daughter. "The people in the Officers Personnel Division had to behave and dress just right. Some of the girls even went to college. One of them, Jessica, was going out with Brian, a Navy lieutenant. They were such a nice couple, very good looking and so classy. I think they got married after the war but I was never in touch after I left that job."

That hit me hard. I was forty years old before I realized how my sister and I got our names in a world of Maries, Anthonys, Franks, and Joes. We were named after an ideal, after real Americans.

There is no one way of being "American." We start on a path. Sometimes we follow the path straight to the end. Sometime we veer off in different directions. On that day at the new WTC, I thought back to 9/11 and all the paths that led so many people to that place on that day.

I don't know exactly what "the American Dream" is. That phrase is an overused term to express a vague generality. Every person's dream is different.

And our dreams are what make us human.

AMERICAN BREAD

By Kenneth J. Uva

It was one of those stores that you find only in Manhattan. Not everywhere in Manhattan. Just in places where people had little shops to sell things they love. There are a few in the Village and in Chelsea and here and there on the Upper West Side. If they can be classified at all, they would be nostalgia shops. Brian walked into one on his lunch hour one work day.

The store was run by two middle- aged men who seemed to be selling the contents of Brian's mother's basement. There were quality items like delicately etched crystal glasses popular in the 40s. More mundane stuff included ash trays and candy dishes in the boomerang shapes and the ever popular turquoise of the 50s. What really caught Brian's eye, however, were objects that he had never seen before even in the most *kitschy* of these emporiums of our former popular culture. In a locked cabinet, along with the white frosted glass tumblers with gold abstract dancing figures sat a set of Welch's Jelly glasses.

Fuck Proust and his madeleines, Brian thought, these bring me back.

Everyone in his old neighborhood drank from glasses that were formerly jars of jelly. The company thoughtfully packaged their grape jelly (seedless, if you please) in jars with a pry-off lid that could be used as drinking glasses. The painted-on pictures were from Disney movies and various cartoons and stories. Mickey and Donald came to mind immediately for Brian. And Howdy Doody. These glasses brought Brian back to his boyhood home and his beloved lunches of peanut butter and jelly on American bread.

"They didn't call it hide and seek. They called it 'hanglo,' 'hanglo seek.'"

Brian was engaging in one of his favorite diatribes, regaling Sophie and Joni about how dumb people were in his old neighborhood. Even though he moved away from the old neighborhood, on the cusp of Brownsville, East New York and Bedford Stuyvesant, almost forty years before, there is something of the old terrain that still stayed with him.

"There were so many stupid people. I hardly ever heard anything intelligent outside my house or the school. That strip of concrete between the sidewalk and the street was the *curve*. They said '*lever* mind.' Did you know there was a song called 'The *Aller* Rose of Texas?' "

"How could anyone…?" Sophie didn't even bother finishing the sentence. To her, the subject was not worthy of further discussion. How could someone of her taste, refinement, and cool, have descended from someone who came from a place like that?

"It's true," Brian said, warming to the subject. "I'm not making this up. This wasn't one of those Jewish neighborhoods where education was everything and people struggled to send their kids to college. These were Italians. No one went to college. No one talked about college. Except your grandmother. I was the smartest kid in the school and she knew I was going to college. Like people did in the movies."

Brian's mother was one of the exceptions in the neighborhood. While firmly rooted in the Italian traditions of family, religion, and macaroni on Sundays, she peeked outward to the larger world. A high school graduate during World War II, when few in the neighborhood were, she was considered a bit stuck up. More than one person said, "She thinks who she is." But there was enough of the Italian in her to see non-Italian things as the "other." So sliced white bread, like Wonder Bread, or local brands like Silvercup, was, to her, American bread. A person, whose parents, unlike her own, were not born in an old country, was an *American*.

Brian was like that in some ways. As a boy, in his head, he was as American as the Beaver, or Davy Crockett. Yet, in his guts, that deep place where you find your true self, there was much of the Italian-Catholic tradition. His wife, Sarah, always said that Jews had the reputation for being morbid and fatalistic. Until she married Brian, she had never known the dark side of Italians. Southern Italians, at least. Maybe it was the long history of poverty and occupation by foreigners, but all that singing and dancing was a crock. These people are dark. Life is sad so don't expect too much. No wonder so many of them named their daughters Lucy, after the saint depicted holding a plate with her eyes on it.

When Brian is telling his daughters about his early youth, before the move to the suburbs when he became a normal American, his outward thrust is the humor about a place that was like no other in America. "Every girl was named Antoinette or Josephine. Their mothers taught them to cook at an early age to be sure they were marriage material. And cooking was a sacred ritual, especially the gravy."

Here is where Sophie stepped into her great lady mode and intoned, "Fortunately, I will have servants and don't have to worry about *that* sort of thing."

Brian continued, on a roll. "I'm not kidding, they called pasta sauce gravy. And everyone had a strong philosophy about how to do it right. Aunt Rose's was no good because she burned the onions. They argued about whether to strain the tomatoes or to leave in the seeds and the pulp."

Joni chimed in. "I can't believe that was so important to people then."

"Joni," Brian replied, "you are a long way from your roots. What do you kids know, anyway, you, who wanted to leave the San Gennaro Feast because you hated the crowds and the smells? The smell of the sausages and onions make my mouth water. I don't eat them, of course, bad for you."

That is Brian. Loves the idea of the old ethnic food but doesn't eat it. Watches his fats, cholesterol, sodium, and general intake. Eats soy products, takes loads of vitamins and herbs, jogs, and doesn't look a bit like the other men who came from the same place and the same time. Comfortable in the Italian part of the Village and the "Bohemian" part, but somehow uneasy in each. Maybe that is because he avoids extremes. Intellectual, but grounded in reality. Forward thinking, but tied to his roots. Traditional, but not when the tradition weighs you down, or keeps you from marrying a Jew.

The tension between the traditional world and the outside world was a subtext of Brian's life. Much of that came from his mother. Her birth name was Carmella. She was named that because she was born on the feast day of Our Lady of Mount Carmel. She hated that name. It was too old world for her. Her friends called her Millie and she used Mildred as her official name all her life. Yet, she *was* different from most of the girls in the neighborhood. She never used foul language, and somehow, everyone knew that you acted differently around Millie. Maybe she took those 30s and 40s movies seriously. Maybe it was possible to go to college and wear college sweaters and know young men who spoke perfect English and had good teeth. Perhaps there were real people who went to swank nightclubs like Fred and Ginger

Brian's old Brooklyn neighborhood was full of regular guys. They read *The Daily News,* often walking to the local candy store to get the late night edition. And, maybe, some of these guys weren't so bad. His father worked for the electric company. Two uncles were automobile mechanics. Two others worked for the Post Office when a job with the Post Office meant something. They took pride in working for the U.S. government. They polished their brass buttons and shined their hat brims. Once, when seeing a black woman mail carrier wearing shorts, Brian commented, only half in jest, "It's a good thing Uncle Frank and Uncle Mike aren't around to see that."

For Brian, the uncle with the best job of all was Uncle Tony. He was a welder at the Brooklyn Navy Yard. They built ships there, large warships. He and thousands of other regular guys, built battleships and aircraft carriers. Even after the peak years of World War II, the place was still active, building large aircraft carriers in case the cold war got hot, or maybe to prevent it from becoming hot. They had visitor days and there was nothing more thrilling for Brian than to visit the place and see the ships docked there and to climb aboard the carriers and submarines. The Russians better not mess with us when we have these ships, thought Brian.

His father was a Navy man in World War II so Brian was partial to the navy as the best branch of the service. The best navy in the world, thought Brian. They sank all those Nazi U-Boats to win the war in Europe. Dad's navy, in the Pacific, kicked the shit out of the Japs, with their sneak attack on Pearl Harbor, *kamikazes*, and *banzai* charges. His father had told Brian all about Okinawa and the Japanese planes crashing into American ships, of being awake for 48 hours straight, staring at this radar screen, and warning the ship of a Japanese bomber heading straight for it, a warning in time for his shipmates to spot the plane and shoot it down. What kind of enemy was this? They committed suicide for their goddamned emperor?

But on our ships and in the air and on the ground there were millions of ordinary American boys, regular guys, from towns and farms and cities. They stood by their guns and their buddies and their flag. Uncle Tony's LST hit a mine and sank at the mouth of the Seine. Uncle Mario was in heavy infantry fighting across France. To this day, he won't talk about it. They fought as free men, no bows to the Emperor or *Heils!* to the Fuhrer. Brooklyn was full of men like these. Brian was proud to be the son of one of them.

When Brian wasn't carrying on about the unique stupidity of so many of the denizens, he would admit that he lived in a special place at a special time. The time was the mid 1950s and as a boy of five, he was not quite aware that he was a witness to history. His father lived and breathed baseball. He was the speedy second baseman of his high school team, taught Brian the game, and loved the Dodgers. Brian liked to play his father's brand of baseball. Neither of them was big, but they were fast and agile. Brian was never the player his father was, but he also played second base, and liked to bunt and steal bases in Little League. That was real baseball, the way God wanted it played. When provoked, Brian would do his act about juiced up balls and bats and bulked up players who were useless except when hitting home runs.

"Ebbets Field was right on the street," Brian explained to Sophie and Joni. "Driving by, I could see the dents that the baseballs made in the chain link fence in right field."

Brian's first sports memory, and maybe the first memory outside his personal experiences, involved the Brooklyn Dodgers. People argued about which of the New York teams was the best–the Dodgers, the Giants, or the Yankees.

"The Yankee fans would always rub it in about how the Dodgers never won a World Series and how the Yankees won every year," he told Joni, who always seemed interested in what he had to say. To the Brooklyn fans, "Wait 'till next year" was the slogan of futility. But, in 1955, it was next year. The Dodgers, finally, beat the Yankees.

"There were parties in the streets," Brian remembered. "People cried and hugged each other." When his father told him that the Dodger center fielder Duke Snider hit four home runs to tie the Series record, he became Brian's idol for the rest of his life. Brian, the cynical intellectual, the man whose language and demeanor never betrayed his roots, made the pilgrimage to Cooperstown 25 years later when the Duke was inducted into the Baseball Hall of Fame.

Brooklyn's glory was short lived. Two year later, in an act of infamy comparable to Pearl Harbor, the Dodger owner, Walter O'Malley, moved the team to Los Angeles.

"Looking back," Brian reflected, "I was really mad that the Dodgers left Brooklyn. It was only later that I realized what else was leaving.

The world of the regular guys was going away. The guys who read *The Daily News* and argued about baseball and worked in the Navy Yard and Con Edison and in the breweries and factories were also leaving. Everyone moved to the suburbs. Brooklyn was changing. Our people were moving out, the 'coloreds' were moving in."

Brian's father was a bit reluctant to move at first. Brooklyn was his world. His job was 20 minutes away by subway or car. You could pick up the evening edition of *The Daily News* at the candy store across the street and run into the guys and shoot the bull for awhile before going home. But he knew it was better for the kids. Brian's mom, however, had been looking outside Brooklyn for some time.

"Everybody worked during World War II, except Francie."

At dinner one night, Brian, was telling Sarah and the girls one of the family legends. In a time when war industries reached deep into the local neighborhoods where, for example, the costume factory worked three shifts making uniforms, everyone worked. Everyone, that is except his father's sister Francie. A healthy young woman in her mid-twenties at the time, she stayed home, cashed the allotment checks three brothers sent to their mother, and leaned out the window resting her elbows on a pillow. The story was told often, as are many family stories. Brian, however, particularly liked that one. He wondered, two generations later, what his daughters might be doing if the country was fully mobilized like in WWII. After the women's rights movement, with women in positions they didn't have in the past, the thought of his aunt being a slacker at the highpoint of The Greatest Generation, amused him.

Carmella, however, was no slacker. A high school graduate, a fine-looking, well-groomed young woman with good typing skills, she landed a job with the Navy Department. She worked in the Officers' Personnel Division. Due to the Navy traditions and hierarchy, this was no ordinary job. Naval officers were gentlemen too and the Navy treated them as such. So the Officers' Personnel Division was staffed by elite secretaries. Brian had seen pictures of the "girls" in that office. Every one of them was attractive and well dressed in the Betty Grable, Andrews Sisters style of the time. Miss Carter, the supervisor, required hats and gloves, no gum chewing, and the most refined deportment at all times.

The Navy Department was an eye opener for Carmella. She worked in the Federal Building in lower Manhattan. So, every day, she rode the subway out of Brooklyn to "New York." She ate lunch with the other young working women at Schrafts on special occasions and the Horn and Hardhart Automat on most regular days. Sure, it wasn't Park Avenue. But it wasn't Brooklyn either. It was, for her, a world of what might be. A world where people dressed nicely, and spoke and acted with some refinement. Was it really possible for someone like her, the only high school graduate out of 6 children, whose parents came to America through Ellis Island, to be a real American? Could she live in a house surrounded by grass? Could her son go to college and wear a white shirt and tie to work? Could her daughter go to college too? Maybe meet and marry a professional man? Maybe all things are possible now that she saw the other side of America.

Brian often wondered, in a world of Anthonys, Joeys, Vinnies, Antoinettes, Josephines, and Maries, how he ended up with his name without actually being Irish. Or how his sister was named Jessica. One day, towards his fortieth birthday, he was chatting with his mother on her patio while watching six-year old Sophie and three-year old Joni splash around in the inflatable kiddie pool his father would set up whenever his grandchildren visited during the summer. The subjects rambled about this and that, people from their presents, and people from their pasts. Brian joked that living in the New York area, he was 21 before he actually saw a natural blonde. That New York is so different from the rest of the country because of all the ethnic groups that he had to trespass to the Upper East Side of Manhattan to actually see people who really looked like the models in *The New York Times Magazine*. It was a familiar light-hearted chat that was really about crossing cultural borders, a subject close to Brian as his education, profession, and experiences moved him ever outward from the Old Neighborhood of his origins.

"Yes," Carmella finally replied. "I remember when I was working in the Navy Department. There was a young officer who dated and was going to marry one of the girls in my office. She was so refined. She grew up in Connecticut, even went to college. She spoke soooo beautifully. Her name was Jessica. He was from Massachusetts. A handsome lieutenant. All of us in the office were so sad when we found out that Brian was killed when his ship was torpedoed in the Pacific."

"Holy shit," Brian thought. He was almost forty and had just learned that his sister Jessica and he were named after two people his mother knew way back when. It was sad, really, but for her, not for him. She gave her children the names of two people idealized for what she thought they represented-- life's wonderful possibilities for those who are true Americans.

Carmella's office with the Navy Department was at 90 Church Street. Later that building stood, literally, in the shadow of the twin towers of the World Trade Center, just across the street. The building was damaged on September 11 but remained intact. The first time Brian was able to get close enough to Ground Zero he thought about his mother, now deceased, working there as a young woman with dreams, about Brian, long dead, and wondered where Jessica was now. And then, looking into the 16-acre hole in the ground where the World Trade Center once stood, thought about all the dead, and the families of the dead, and their stories and their dreams, and about the fate brings people to a certain place at a certain time. All colors and religions, and attitudes and hopes, optimists and pessimists, lucky and unlucky, strong and weak, heroes known and unknown, living their lives, trying to realize a measure of happiness.

This is America, Mother.

Brian shed a tear, and moved on.

The Fall of the House of Amato

By Kenneth Uva

"Hey, Joey, we're playin stickball on Dean Street, c'mon," Tony proclaimed loud enough to be heard by all the kids playing in the street. It was also heard by the older guys hanging around, and the old ladies sitting in front of their houses in folding chairs. Dressed in mourning black most of the time, the ladies watched the goings on in their small corner of East New York. They judged and were ready to report any breaches of any of the codes lived by the residents of their villages in Italy. These codes, now transplanted to Brooklyn, did not deviate much from what they brought from the old country.

"I don't wanna play on Dean Street. Let's go round the corner. It's better there," was Joey's reply.

The reason that it was better around the corner was that Dean Street was where the Amato family lived and Joey was tired of the teenage daughters, Mary and Carmella, always asking Joey and his brothers to help them with something or run an errand.

The patriarch of Amato clan was Antonio, known as "the General." He was well-established in his East New York neighborhood by the time Joey's mother and father arrived from the Puglia region of Italy in 1907. Joey's family, the Gallos, was related to the Amatos through Joey's mother, whose aunt Regina was married to the General. The link of the families though blood was augmented by the fact that the General owned the building where the Gallos lived, thus the dual link of family (blood) and money.

Antonio and Regina had four children. The oldest, Antonio, Jr. was also known as "Junior." His younger brother Jimmy was a meek, quiet type, unusual in that tough neighborhood. Mary and Carmella were known for looking down on the other neighborhood kids for not having nice clothes or for the status of being the General's daughter.

In addition to owning several small buildings of between three and six apartments, the main source of the Amato fortune was the Amato Funeral Home. Despite the low income of the neighborhood, the fact that people died regardless of the demographics assured a steady income.

The General, along with a few of the other more prosperous of the recent immigrants from area around Bari, Italy, contributed money, ideas, and physical labor into building Saint Anthony's Roman Catholic Church. The church was built in the early 1900s to meet the needs of the growing Italian population of the neighborhood in an era when the Catholic churches reflected the ethnic makeup of the area. The older nearby church, Blessed Sacrament, was built by the Germans who preceded the Italians in populating that area of Brooklyn before Brooklyn was consolidated into Greater New York. In contrast to the stark, tan brick interior of Blessed Sacrament, Saint Anthony was designed in a faux Baroque design, light blue and white interior with reproductions of Renaissance paintings on the sides of the altar and painted wooden saints, with graphic wounds, and one of Saint Lucy holding a plate containing her eyes, representing an account of her torture by eye gouging. The gruesome stories of the Christian martyrs in the time of the Roman Empire make for disturbing reading to say the least.

The Amatos were definitely the most prominent family in the neighborhood. They had a great influence on what was considered proper behavior. The General and his associates connected with the church determined who would be allowed to sell their wares and food at the annual St. Anthony's Day feast. They had the pull to have the city close the street adjacent to the school yard so the various merchants could set up their booths. The main attraction was the food—zeppoli, sausage and peppers, pasta ("macaroni") with sauce ("gravy") that most often resulted in the neighborhood women saying that they made all of that better at home. Dining out, even on the street where they lived, was not a popular activity for people with limited financial resources and a narrow view of what was good to eat.

While the official memory of the era was that Italian-Americans were loyal to the United States, there was still a major connection to the homeland. When Mussolini's army conquered Ethiopia as part of the dictator's plan to extend Italy's dominance in parts of Africa, there was a great deal of support for this aggression in the neighborhood. The General, with others, organized a parade to commemorate Italy's victory. Along with the church sponsored marching band, an African-American man who worked in the funeral home was seated in a coffin with a sign around his neck reading *"Qui giance Abyssinia"* ("Here lays Ethiopia").

When Joey was a few years older and in the Navy in the South Pacific, he received a letter from his sister Christina. The General and the church arranged for a dance for the Italian POWs. The tone of the letter was that this was a great thing, so nice that the church did something for these young prisoners. Joey was outraged that he and so many of the neighborhood boys were fighting the enemy and the enemy solders were being entertained by the church and the neighborhood girls. Later, Joey told his son Brian that he was so mad about this and realized how stupid his sister was for not realizing how this news would be received by the boys serving overseas.

Along with Joey in the navy, his brothers Al and Pete were in the army. Al was a combat infantryman in Europe. He saw heavy combat and returned carrying those experiences with him for the rest of his life. It was hard to get him to talk about the war, leaving to the imagination what he saw and, possibly, what he did in his fight against the Germans in France and Belgium. Pete was an Army Air Corps mechanic repairing fighter planes at various training bases in the South. Junior Amato escaped the draft since he was married, a father, and a bit older than the average draftee. Jimmy was declared unfit for military service for reasons not known by the Gallo family.

When the war ended, the Gallo brothers returned to the neighborhood. Older and more confident due to their service in the victorious war effort, they felt less like the poor cousins but not yet equal in the feudal order to the Amato clan.

By the time the Gallo boys came back, the General had died. Junior now was in charge of the funeral home. Jimmy did some of the paper work but never acted like a boss even though, technically, he was part owner. Mary and Carmella were dating, trying to find men good enough to merge with the Amato dynasty.

In the years shortly after World War II, the Gallo brothers all married and no longer lived in the building owned by the Amatos, although their mother still did. So, there was not yet a complete break from the ties that had, for four decades, bound the Gallos to the Amatos. The Amato clan certainly thought the ties continued.

Joey was married to Betty, who he had met in high school. She was also from the neighborhood and also Italian American. When Betty's mother died, her father did not use the services of the Amato Funeral Home. Years before, during the Great Depression, the owner of the Lombardi Funeral Home had loaned Betty's father money when he was having a tough time with his furniture business. "Mr. Lombardi did me a big favor twenty years ago. I repay him by having Momma's funeral at his funeral parlor. That is the honorable thing to do."

Apparently, the Amatos, especially, the sisters Mary and Carmella, did not consider this honorable at all. "Wha s'amatter, they too good for us? After all we did for the Gallos?" The fact that it wasn't the Gallos but Joey's father in law, who made that decision, didn't matter a bit. They carried a grudge forever.

Mary and Carmella married and had children in the years after the war. None seemed to reach the high status that the Amato clan was used to. There was some spotty education that they didn't talk about. There were no prestigious jobs or careers or they would have bragged about that. Yet, they still tried to find ways to be able to look down on the Gallo family.

At a family function that was extensive enough for the Amatos to be invited, Betty told her son Brian that Mary and Carmella always try to find something bad about the Gallos. "They are very frustrated about their lives and their husbands and children. They will try to get something about the Gallos that they could use against us," Betty explained. "If they ask you anything about your job, just say it is good, you like it." Brian, who by this time was a lawyer in the early stages of his career and had never met the "Amato girls" so he had no idea of the underlying plot in this family gathering. He took heed of this mother's warnings, not wanting to give the Amatos ammunition to use against his family. He turned to his sister Jessica who was sitting next to him. "I never even met these people and someone I feel I am in the middle of a battle between the Medici and the Borgias."

Sure enough both Mary and Carmella approached Brian. "You are Joey's son, right? Mary asked. Carmella chimed in, "You're the lawyer?" "Yes, I'm a lawyer," Brian replied. The next question was the inevitable one of what kind of law do you practice. Brian explained that he worked for a company in Manhattan and handled things like contracts and claims. "I guess you would like to do something better," Mary said, obviously insinuating that Brian was unhappy in his job. Since Brian was clued into what was going on, he responded: "I am really happy with where I am and what I'm doing. I supervise five other attorneys. My company does business in every state and has offices in all the major cities. I get to deal with matters and with people from all over the country. It's a great job and look forward to going to work every day."

Brian did not love his job but realized that this wasn't a situation that called for a complicated discussion involving the business atmosphere, the corporate culture and the day to day stress he had to deal with. He knew that any slightly negative inference would be rebroadcast, as "Joey's son, the lawyer, doesn't like his job and wants to find another one."

As years went on, the Amatos became less and less important in the lives of the Gallos. Some member of the Gallo family would invite the Amatos to major family functions such as weddings and some did not. Joey and Betty did not invite them to the weddings of Brian or Jessica and, in fact, Brian heard nothing about that clan until much later when he visited Joey, now retired. "Junior had his driver take him here last week. He said that his son Michael was in trouble with the mob and they need five thousand dollars or they will kill him. He said he would give me a note. Can you write one?" Brian said he could do that but did his father really want to lend Junior money? After all, Junior was not his brother. Brian realized that Joey wanted to show that after all the years of the Amatos acting superior to the Gallos, for all their pretensions and airs, an Amato is coming to him in order to save his son's ass. "It's not the money," Joey said. "I have plenty but they can't raise five thousand between the whole bunch." Brian drafted the note; Junior signed it, and received the money.

Two years later, Junior died. Joey contacted Michael and asked to be repaid. "There is no money. Guys we owed took over the funeral home. Sorry, Joey."

So that was that, after decades of being the richest family in the neighborhood, looking down on others, acting as the local nobility long after they had the resources to do so, the house of Amato was broke and powerless. The entire estate could not yield five thousand dollars to honor a debt made in order to save one of their lives.

Like the Ambersons, the Amatos received their comeuppance.

Made in the USA
Middletown, DE
06 January 2023